PRAISE FOR RICHARD STERN'S *STITCH*

"Richard Stern is a very serious novelist. He has a talented ear, he has equipment for complicated comic apprehensions, he is caring, and he is dedicated."—Marcus Klein, *The Reporter*

"Moving and intelligent at once . . . every word right. And the best most decent thing ever written about Pound."—Karl Shapiro

"A beautifully written and ironic book."—Day Thorpe, *Washington Star*

"A new Ulysses book is with us. . . . Edward is a man worthy of creation by Joyce or the Henry James of 'The Beast in the Jungle.' —Harry Cargas, *St. Louis Globe-Democrat*

"A gem of high wit written by a master of the language."—Thomas Berger

"*Stitch* tells the truth, and of course, more than the truth. The emotion is fully there. . . . Stern's best book."—Bernard Malamud

"The book goes through the mind's eye as rich and infolded as Venice itself."—Herbert Blau

"An allusive book, a brilliant playing on surfaces. . . . A strange technique, fascinating. Tact! Grace!"—George P. Elliott

"Always a virtue, his precision shows no blurring. . . . *Stitch* has muscle and tone."—*Book Week*

"When *Stitch* was first published I heard vague rumblings and grumblings in my parents' entourage, but I stayed clear of it and did not get to see the book. I had read *In Any Case* in 1963, perhaps too hurriedly thinking: aha, another American traveling through Europe,

T0057586

learning language to find his own and himself. The usual onion without a core? No. I was able to bridge the deep gulch between our logistics during the war as soon as I read: 'no one can hate invaders as farmers can.' A straightforward statement. Despite my distaste for the 'Intelligence,' the father-son search had fascinated me. In 1997, thanks to my friend Miriam, I saw Richard Stern in Chicago. I confessed I had never read *Stitch*. He gave me a copy. I promptly agree with Frank MacShane: yes, it takes courage to write a novel set in Venice. After Baron Corvo, Henry James, Thomas Mann, and D'Annunzio, too many contemporary writers have used Venice as a mere backdrop for facile crime or social tit for tat. In a different category, in 2001 appeared *Parsifal a Venezia* by the Pythagorean composer-conductor, born in Venice, Giuseppe Sinopoli. The 'tetraktus' is incomplete. The lines laid out by *Stitch* are missing. Fiction or nonfiction, each step is exact. I can find my way to Calle Querini, to 'Cicci' and to San Michele. Richard Stern is a thoughtful man. He truly cares for his subject. Others have spoken of his brilliance, intelligence, wit. I admire his humaneness. He writes with compassion. The author of *Stitch* has a heart, he has reached his pure, solid core."—Mary de Rachewiltz

"*Stitch* is strangely moving."—*Fort Worth Texas Press*

STITCH

BOOKS BY RICHARD STERN

STITCH

Richard Stern

Foreword by Ingrid D. Rowland

TriQuarterly Books
Northwestern University Press
Evanston, Illinois

TriQuarterly Books
Northwestern University Press
Evanston, Illinois 60208-4170

Northwestern University Press edition published 2004. Foreword copyright
© 2004 by Ingrid D. Rowland. Copyright © 1965 by Richard Stern. First
published in 1965 by Harper & Row. All rights reserved.

Printed in Canada

10 9 8 7 6 5 4 3 2 1

ISBN 0-8101-5148-0

Library of Congress Cataloging-in-Publication data are available from the
Library of Congress.

The paper used in this publication meets the minimum requirements of the
American National Standard for Information Sciences—Permanence of Paper
for Printed Library Materials, ANSI Z39.48-1992.

for Andrew, with love

Foreword to the New Edition

Ingrid D. Rowland

In the nearly forty years since the initial publication of Richard Stern's *Stitch,* the novel's basic human themes have changed not at all, but the Venice in which his characters play out their lives has changed—in some respects, drastically. It is not only that public transportation is now run by a group called ENAV rather than ACNIL, or that the doorbells of the 1960s still involved bells and cords rather than the electronic *citofoni* that succeeded them. The whole composition of the city itself has changed in the course of a generation. Those frugal families who made up the Venetian working class have long since moved in masses to the mainland, leaving behind more and more of Venice itself to a luxurious, and luxuriant, tourist trade. Shops now purvey mostly carnival masks, Murano glass, colored silks, artistic paper, and clothing made by the same international designers who can be found in any major city around he world. Gondoliers sing Neapolitan songs to their fares. Docile crowds line up to see the interior of San Marco or the latest show at Palazzo Grassi, largely indifferent to the fact that one is a working cathedral and the other a museum. A more deliberately artistic subset, thinner and more likely to be dressed in black, lines up around the Fascist-era pavilions now used for the Biennale or down the narrow calli leading to the Peggy Guggenheim Collection, no longer a home. Banners flap from palazzi on the Grand Canal to announce everything from Biennale shows to museums to restoration projects. Venice is still beautiful enough to be a dream, but it no longer harbors nearly as many penniless dreamers as it did in the optimistic, destitute sixties. Like the rest of Italy, it has grown richer and sleeker, and the young dreamers have moved on to Prague and other places where people are still poor enough to share.

And yet, some things never change: the huge, architectonic piles of Tiepolo clouds still hover over the lagoon; the jeweled façades of the palazzi on the Grand Canal still sprout their filigree carving; long-nosed cats with close-set eyes still maintain their distinctively Venetian faces; Titian, Veronese, and Tintoretto still make looking at painting an experience in touch; and where else could a philosopher be elected mayor, as Massimo Cacciari was in the 1990s? The backdrop of *Stitch,* the city that constitutes the novel's real protagonist, is still recognizably itself, old enough to have seen nearly everything several times over, beautiful enough to endow everything that happens there with a sense of importance, filled enough with works of genius, or at least of supreme competence, to awaken ambitions that would lie happily dormant anywhere else.

Against this Venetian backdrop, a small group of Americans plays out one year in their lives: Edward, the hapless ad man whose desires in this most seductive of cities have become as uncontrollable as his girth; Nina, the aspiring writer who lives by cadging food, lodging, toothbrushes, and underwear; and Stitch, a personage so large that his name in the book's title is all capitals, the great sculptor whose character and history—everything, in fact, except his chosen art form—are closely based on Stern's own Venetian encounters with Ezra Pound. It is not quite right to call these characters expatriates, because Edward and his family will return home as scheduled, and Nina is a bird of passage, perpetually en route, aware that what drives her is less the urge to stay in Venice than the urge to write—although Venice gives her living and writing a particular focus. She has a real creator's capacity for discipline and self-sacrifice, but she is not mature enough yet to know whether she will survive as a devotee to the writer's life.

As for Stitch, the things that he has done and endured transcend nationality; he is, if anything, a refugee in Venice. Like Pound, Stern's Stitch has collaborated with the Fascists in Italy, for which he has spent ten years in prison rather than being confined, as Pound was, to a mental institution. This slight alteration of real history allows Stern to focus on imprisonment as the essential point in Stitch's formation as an artist rather than the more complicated issues that Pound's detention raised—and raises—about the boundaries between madness, genius, and solipsism. Stitch is fully, unquestionably sane, and he is a more heroic and more novelistic figure than Pound. Hence, as a sculptor, he creates an art that communicates more directly to humanity at large than Pound's often hermetic poetry; Stern's hero has spent decades transforming an island in the Venetian lagoon into a carved narrative of universal history, reshaping nature much as the Venetians once shaped their gorgeous city from the shifting silt of a swamp. Only Venice itself, the almost human city, has the breadth of experience to grant Stitch real pardon for his real errors and sympathize in full with his project to make a lasting object in the middle of a lagoon. But Venice also induces each of the other characters to grant Stitch forbearance for the huge sins his gifts have led him to commit. The chronically overwhelmed, silly Edward redeems himself as the person through whom Stern takes on the question of Pound's anti-Semitism with acuity and compassion. Stitch's island, meanwhile, is shown to us through the eyes of Nina, who, unlike Edward, all desire and no will, commands enough will of her own to understand something of the terrible tribute that Stitch has offered to his art. Readers will have to make do with imagining Stitch's island, but in essence it must look very much like his adopted city. As Stern writes: "it is Venice itself—the sum of a thousand years of creativity holding up against falsity and nature's pounding—that challenges, excites, appeases and consoles the protagonists," and this stubborn will to invention is what Stitch must ultimately have been driven to portray in sculpture.

Happily, Venice, and this series of intertwined stories about the curious, earnest characters who inhabit it for four seasons, can now also challenge, excite, appease, and console a new generation of readers; if anything, the changes that have transformed postwar Italy into a great power and altered the conditions of life in Venice only serve to confirm the essential timelessness of Stern's novel.

◈ chapter 1

THE VAPORETTO to the Giudecca which Edward usually caught at night left the San Zaccaria pier at 11:59, an odd time which magnified his fear of missing it and having to hang around the Riva for another hour. He needed fifteen good minutes to reach it from Santa Maria del Giglio, his pace an alternate dash and fast walk. If the Piazza were clear, the dashes came off, and he was there with a couple of minutes to spare, the ACNIL men raising their hands to slow him up as he lumbered over the bridge in front of the Danieli. Despite the mounting weight he applied to Venetian scales (none accurate, but all in accord about his piling flesh), his running improved through October, but in November, high water in the Piazza and around the bridges slowed him up three or four minutes, hopping on his heels through the water and, in the Piazza, jumping from table to table on the overpass. Once or twice he caught the boat just as the ropes were unwound from the iron stanchions.

STITCH

The Thursday before what would be Thanksgiving Day in the States—the Gunthers hadn't remembered until McGowan, the foolish, lascivious consul, had said he'd bring them a turkey from the PX in Vicenza—Edward met not only the risen water but a terrific fog which blindfolded the town and forced him into tentative groping through streets and over bridges until the Piazza, where he loped, arm stiffened in front of him for interference. The great breadth of the Piazza was scarcely a gauze of light, and the Campanile, which usually loomed up in front of him like the Empire State Building, was a vague guess of stone within the general death of distinction. By the time his hand was feeling its way around the great pillars of the Ducal Palace the midnight bells were sounding, first San Zaccaria's, then the baritone Marangona from the Campanile, even that blurred by the fog. "I've missed it." A foghorn groaned over the invisible lagoon.

Above the ticket window, a sign said there'd be no boats crossing till the fog lifted; the ACNIL man inside guessed it would be hours. Edward sat on the pier rail, shivering and sweating, wiping his head with his yellow scarf, taking long breaths and working to get the thump in his chest below auditory level. In the icy, edgeless cotton, the wind lifted the gondolas out against their ropes in the watery pens, and the ropes, slipping up and down, drew moans from the stakes. "Stuck."

He walked back where he'd run, more or less intending to head for the Zattere on the other side of town where traghettos went across to the Giudecca every half hour, fog or not, but by the time he was at the Palace, feeling his way from pillar to pillar, he'd decided to go back to Nina's.

At Santa Maria del Giglio, he turned up the calle, rang her bell, answered the *"Chi è"* with "Just me again," and ran up the flight, her new pooch, Charley, a gondolier's gift, at his ankles. "Fog. No boats." She was still in sweater and skirt. He took off his coat and shoes and lay down on her backbreaking couch-bed. "No sleep tonight?"

"You're not the only guest of the evening."

Could it be? "I am sorry, Nina." He went for his shoes. "I'll get out."

"Stay put. No evacuation necessary. There'll be tea in a minute. I wouldn't have let you back in if there were anything awkward."

Perhaps it was a girl. He should certainly put on his shoes, pull up his tie. But why hadn't she told him before?

Nina went into the kitchenette, a small square off the low slot which was bedroom, sitting room and study, three straight chairs, a four-tiered bookshelf, a table covered with papers, pencils, books, magnifying glass, file cards, colored prints of the Schifanoia frescoes, a Pevsner study, a fourteenth-century zodiac, a shaggy dog's rug, the bed. A place like something worn to keep out cold; dark and snug. She was back with a plate of cookies and tarts. "We're really putting on the dog. Who is it?"

The bell sounded. She pulled the admission cord without calling *"Chi è."* "You'll see now."

There weren't more than twenty steps to the flight, but it was a minute before the other guest arrived, a large gray-bearded man, wrapped in a black cloak, his huge gray head barely topped by a black corduroy fedora. He nodded to Nina and, after an introduction to Edward, took off the cape and hat and

[3]

dropped them into the armchair by the end of the couch where Edward now sat, his feet feeling past Charley's snout for his shoes under the coffee table. Meanwhile Edward was digesting the name with the man. The famous firebrand was hardly glowing. Yet so familiar was the face even in the first minute that Edward felt that he'd somehow sensed who it was from the slow ascent of the stairs. Impossible, but such was his consciousness of Stitch's presence in Italy and of his great work here in Venice. "I suppose I should have guessed you might be here," familiarity driving through awe. "I went out to your island the second day."

Stitch, at the other end of the couch, examined Edward through deep, small, greenly brilliant eyes, a ferret's through a thicket, then, in a soft, burry voice said, "A few other things in Venice have priority, I believe."

A stopping remark. Not offensive, not aggressive, but conclusive. The demur was both modest and immodest, a truth, yet an invitation to denial. Perhaps even an appeal for denial. It was followed by a block of silence incised by Nina's kitchen noises. Edward felt its burden so heavily it took him a minute to raise it with a question of how long Stitch had been in Venice.

The response was a while getting said. "Sixty-eight years." Another stopping remark. Edward could figure no way around or through it, and until Nina brought in tea and passed cookies, he perspired, tense and still. Stitch did not seem bothered by silence. Nina pumped out talk of the fog, the *acque alte,* the early cold, small social noises which, with the tea-drinking sounds, filled the room. Stitch nodded, smiled, drank. Although his silence was a conspicuous social obstacle, Edward felt it entirely natural. Indeed, his initial impression of Stitch was that he had never seen such natural absorption in the immediate occasion. It made the room somehow condense around him, and yet, what could be less assertive than the old futzer sitting there munching cookies?

He munched because of his teeth, six or eight discolored spurs. Maybe they accounted for his silence. Or was it that he had talked too much in his time? Ten years in the jug. My God, thought Edward, to think I'm in the very room with him. He worked now to get back into the conversation and was just managing a question when Stitch got up. Maybe I just thought I asked it. No, he'd heard the words sounding in the room: "Are you working on the island these days?" Was it while he was asking, or just after, that Stitch rose and, without a word, picked up his hat and cape, thanked Nina, and then nodded to Edward with the sweet smile which canceled the harshness of silence. Edward rose, bowed, and took a step that cracked his shin against the coffee table which had trapped one of his shoelaces. When Stitch was out the door, he said, "Ow," and massaged it. It looked as if pain were to be his only souvenir. Was this converse with the great?

"Why didn't you tell me?" He kicked off his shoes and lay back, feet where Stitch had sat; which itself was oddly thrilling.

"What's there to tell? It's his third tea up here. He likes night walking and has no place to go but the place he lives. I met him at Bicci's. I knew he was somebody the second I saw him. He's a nice old fellow. And sort of abandoned."

"Like the Campanile's abandoned? Having nobody to talk with? Is that it?"

"In a way." She reached for glasses stored behind her books on the desk and filled them with Vecchia Romagna.

"*Is* he working here?"

"I ask him nothing at all. I don't think he's up to anything but an occasional walk. It must be cold as Antarctica on that island. I don't ask him and he doesn't tell me anything."

"What's he know about you?"

"What's there to know, Edward? He asked what I did, I read him some poems. He said he liked them. That's it. He's a receptive person. You can tell that."

"I'm sorry I drove him away."

"He's never stayed more than half an hour. He likes night walks. He's recovering from a prostate operation. I get this from Miss Fry."

"*Chi è?*"

"That's the woman he lives with here. There's also a wife in the States. And a child or two by each. They're all supposed to get along. Not exactly the Swiss Family Robinson."

Nina was not as easy as her account. The small jaw was set where the mouth lines curved toward it. She's unsteady about him, thought Edward. Doesn't know how she feels. And as usual, when someone he liked talked about someone else, he was both jealous and embarrassed by his jealousy. Of course prostatitis did not enable felicitous romance. No, that was not it. It was Nina's knowing someone who really counted.

"It makes something special of this place," he said. She laughed. "You know, discarding its specialness." Another from her; she was a big laugher. The blue eyes and flopping dark bangs, the whole round face had the in-and-out action of surprised pleasure. "Discounting you."

Quickly, "I wouldn't count much on *him*."

He sighted her over his dark-socked feet. What was the import of that? "For what? What have I to count on from him?"

"Stimulation. A natural expectancy. But I think he's had it. If he ever had something to get had. I don't know. I know only his reputation. I suppose I've seen three or four of his pieces, but I'm no judge of sculpture. One looked, one liked. I don't know this thing on the island. I mean to go out but it's been too cold. What's it like?"

"I didn't go out. I meant to, but I didn't. I don't know why I said it. It's one of the first things you think of here, and I did think of it the second day. I'll have to go out now. Maybe we ought to go together." After more than a month of seeing her nearly every day he was not yet at ease with her, and this registered in the invitation, which feared and thus invited refusal. But to see the island with Nina would be something more than seeing it with the children and Cressida.

"I'd like to later when it's warmer. For all I know, it may have something to do with what I'm after."

"Which is what, Neen?" Humbly, for he had not heard her talk about her intentions.

Indeed Nina told no one of them. Never seek to tell thy love. Yet, since she'd met him here five weeks before, he'd become part of that group scattered over years and space to whom she'd opened up. "A kind of woman's epic. Not the adventurer founding a city or knocking one over. No justifying, no bragging. Something else." Which was enough.

Her voice had an odd authority; a staking out of territory. It ruffled him enough so that he decided he would not spend the night on her dog's rug nor take the hard little couch, though her offer was genuine if somewhat assertively stoical. He bundled up, kissed her on the lips—which were cold but amiable—and headed for the Zattere.

[7]

STITCH

2

"Whew," she said when the door closed, for she thought tonight might be his pitch and she would run the risk of premature estrangement. He was an unstable mixture of sensitivity and opacity. One could wound him in fifty ways while assuaging him in ten. Perhaps the presence of Stitch had doused his ardor. Despite a certain comfort she got from his kiss, more would have made a fearful mess. The contagious instability of pleasure.

Cleaning up, she stepped an inch short of another consequence of Stitch's presence, the pooch's droppings. He knew what he'd done and shivered behind the wastebasket. "Char-LEY," and she went for him, the newspaper rolled, and he caught a shot on the nose as he beat it, slipping between rugs, sliding under the bed. She cleaned off his mess and tossed it out the window into the canal. "I'll mess you, you son of a bitch," and went after him, dragged him out, lifted and cradled him, kissed where she'd hit, rubbed his stiff little pate, tangled her fingers in the gray-white curls. "Charley, Charley lambchen, what am I gonna do wit ya? Huh? Huh, babykin?" and she put him at the bottom of the bed and rubbed away his trembling. Sad little flesh, affection so carefully installed in it.

Lights out, in pajamas, her foot pressing Charley's stomach from under the quilt, Nina assessed her human friends, Stitch and Edward. Two more different specimens could not easily be produced.

Stitch was the more ponderable, the least available, though somehow linked with her in a way Edward could not be. It was not merely his being an artist. Nor a fellow exile. Nor was it his being a container of precious memories, though the fact that he had known Valéry and Yeats and Blok and Rilke, and their equivalents in building, painting and music, *was* a kind of miracle. As was the fact that he himself belonged to them. With him, the link was something felt even before she'd known who he was.

That her first sight of him had been in the almost isolated Piazza was perhaps a sign of the linkage; nothing between them. It had been the first snow of the year, a very early one which had scuttled the last guides and postcard vendors. The snow piled for half an inch or more on the eaves and cornices of the arcades, lace on the dusk. The Piazza was wonderfully still, as if the snow had joined the universal drive toward inanition. The reduction of movement to ornament. The snow was no quilt, no pile of jewels, no cotton field, only this lacing emphasis of what was already there. She'd been standing under the arches near the loggia of the Campanile, the cold working through her coat, looking. Then she was aware of two people walking in the center of the Piazza, a large man with a cane and a woman in a black cloth coat. The man had a beard, walked slowly, without sureness; the woman seemed to be guiding him by the elbow. Now and then the woman's head tilted to the man's. Nina watched them walk through the archways under the Correr, and knew she'd seen someone special.

Two days later in Bicci's she saw them at a table. They sat silent, he in a brown knit shirt and gray sweater. Her hair was flour-white but she looked young, pretty, good-humored. His face was less overt. The features were distinct yet somehow be-

fogged by wrinkles; he looked remote; he even seemed unaware of the prodigious tangles of pasta he shoveled into his
mouth. When Bicci bobbed over to her table in his day's gaga
round of the customers, she asked him to get them to sign the
guest book, she believed they were *gente importantissime.*
Bicci, in appearance and intellectual development a torsoed
egg, went off for the book; perhaps the old gentleman was a
professore.

Thaddeus Stitch. Lucia Fry.

In Bicci's the next day she'd nodded to them and received
warm smiles in return. Two days later her entering smile was
met with a wave from Stitch, and when she approached, he
rose and held out a chair for her.

During the meal she and Miss Fry did the talking. A hearty
charmer, Miss Fry was fine-spirited, witty, down-to-earth. Like
Stitch, she was an American who'd spent most of her life in
Europe. They both had accents which seemed English, though
Stitch's was burred with Irish sounds.

By the end of the meal they knew that she was a poet, poor,
and like themselves, a long-time emigrée. This without asking.
Miss Fry said they'd noticed how pretty she was, and thought
she must be Irish, they had had many Irish friends over the
years. Nina, imagining what fine company this put her in,
unloosed reminiscence. The "pretty" brought an account of
the Callahan girls, Milly, "the beauty," Aggie, "the wit," Dora,
"the brain." They'd had trouble with Nina. Her most notable
quality was strength. She could stand on her head or on either
hand, lift someone twice her weight. *Intra muros* and behind
the maternal back she became "The Muscle." As for the Irish,
she told of her father's distaste for the label. He was a gentleman, and in his unique view gentlemen had no background.

At any rate, it served to send him into the attic when her mother's professional Irish family poured into the house. There he sat in vest, coat and tie on the seatless frame of an old rocker glaring at the street till the last trace of Erin left the house. Which evoked from Stitch "Emma Bovary," and Nina saw, in a fine flash, yes, this was Francis L., the displaced romantic engulfed by crudity.

"Tell Miss Callahan about Cocteau in his attic."

"You remember better than I, Lucia," the bright, forest-prowler's eyes sinking down somewhere.

"No, I can't possibly," and turning to Nina, "Do ask him? It's a marvelous story."

Nina smiled, shrugged. Stitch settled by muttering something about Cocteau acting the Annunciation with Picasso as the Angel, then retreated into an almost visible silence abandoned only when he paid for Nina's lunch, easily refusing her refusal.

So it began, a couple of weeks in which she went to tea and supper at their small house four times and twice brought them to her room. Then one night, as she was in bed, the bell had sounded, and in answer to her "*Chi è?*" the answer came, "It's I," and she'd had time to slip a sweater and slacks over her pajamas in the minute it took Stitch to climb the stairs.

He did not let her help him with his things, removing the great cape and corduroy fedora while hoping that she did not mind, he was passing, saw her light, and wondered if she had a cup of tea for him.

She was, she said, about to make herself one, and went off to boil water, leaving him with Charley, oddly tranquil under his long, stiff fingers.

When she came back with the pot, Stitch was reading her

one-volume Chaucer. At the coffee table, the teacup at his lips, he regarded her full in the face and said in his clear, quiet, lilting speech, "You radiate peace and inner harmony, Nina."

After a moment she said that this was a kind thing to say to someone. She felt rather at peace but did not know that this was so good a thing. "It may be that I've left too much out."

In the half-light from her wall lamp, a bulb behind a punctured metal hemisphere, his beard and hair gleamed around his smile. He recited:

> Upon hir cheere he wolde him ofte avise,
> Commending in his herte hir wommanhede.
> And eek hir vertu, passing any wight
> Of so yong age, as wel in cheere as deede.

"You're a *galantuomo*."

"He knew how to put things. Transmission is easy when occasion's discovered."

"Griselda is a man's version, but I grant its beauty. And appreciate the beautiful transmission. When do sculptors find time to learn Middle English?"

"When they know precious little else and can't put that to use any more."

Nina felt some excess in the deprecation, but rose to it. "There's enough on record to make that dubious." Which brought a different smile, that of a boy praised by a hard teacher. A surprising turn. "I wish I had some good cakes for you," she said to divert it. "How about bread and *confiture? Framboise.*"

A nod. Charley was in his lap when she returned with the

plate. He broke off a piece for the dog, then asked if she wouldn't read him something of her own.

She read him a canzone she'd written in Paris.

His reaction was ideal, a fine pause, heavy with thought but easy in manifest pleasure. Then, "You have music in you, Nina."

She had never heard anything like that. Francis L. had the force but not the discrimination. "I wish I had more. I feel a starvation in the reprise."

After a silent moment, full for her, he dropped Charley on the floor and got up. "Thank you. I'll come again, if I may. The night air is good discipline for me. After an outing, I can do better what I now do best."

She said she too would sleep well. His praise was grafted upon her confidence, and by the time she heard the downstairs door click shut she felt herself a new person because of it. She had been recognized by someone in the great tradition. It was the first external indication that she belonged there herself.

3

Nina's initial survival in Venice depended on local sympathy for young foreign women and the habit of charging expenses to seldom-dispatched bills. From the time she left the train for her first gape at the water city until she settled off Campo Santa Maria del Giglio ten days later, her weasling appeals for advice, help, and exchanges (of sketches for meals, smiles for coffee and pastry) had linked with flawless fortuity.

The first ten days she stayed two calli from the station in a ratty apartment house which doubled as bead factory. The occupants received the bead supply on Sunday and worked it into a box of necklaces by the next Saturday. Between necklaces, Nina's landlord, Signor Priuli, waited at the station beyond the line of uniformed hotel steerers. When impoverished-looking types passed up the barrage of official offers, Signor Priuli advanced a mustache-shadowed smile and inquired "Rum? *Tsimmer? Shambre? Camera?*" Approached, he explained in Italian and gestures that it was nearby and cheap, a thousand lire a night, or in the *stagione turistica,* fifteen hundred. Nina had been prepared to try hotels, one by one until terms were made she could meet, but a look at Signor Priuli showed her her temporary destination. The choice proved expert: when the little apartment off S.M. del Giglio turned up and Nina gave the Priulis a farewell option of being paid when she got money or of having a charcoal sketch done of a grandson, they opted for the latter. Not from suspicion that there wasn't even a bush to conceal two birds, but because, as good Venetians, they knew that value was appearance and that little counted more than its commemoration.

Nina did not move from the Priulis' on her old principle that mobility was the gentlest mode of defrauding, but because for the first time in her poetic life she had fallen into a bit of financial luck. On the ninth day of her Venetian stay she picked up her first mail at American Express (forwarded from Rome where she'd worked at the Vatican Library and tutored at the American School) and found in it a contract from the University of Oklahoma Press for five hundred dollars. Half-delirious, she staggered into the Piazza, contract in hand, pigeons and tourists sidestepping her. She could not remember the reason anyone should offer her a contract. Sitting at Quadris for her only self-financed drink at a Piazza café during her time in Venice, the delirium parted and the reason came to her. It was for a proposal comparing the early poets of Greece and Italy which, six months ago, she'd written up and sent to five American publishers, all of whom but Oklahoma had said no promptly. That this shot in the dark should result in munificence wrapped in a delightful letter of editorial discernment caused Nina's whole assessment of art and commerce to alter.

Nina's earnings from poetry had been zero. Her sole book was a financial disaster, not of course for her, but for the San Francisco printer of wedding invitations whom she'd persuaded to raise himself into class publishing on her shoulders. Of four hundred copies printed, two hundred lay in the printer's basement. The other two hundred received neither reviews, notice of publication, nor acknowledgment of receipt. Nothing.

Contrast between that polar silence and the shot-in-the-dark confidence from Oklahoma staggered her. In the glaze of morning sun she sat in the great Piazza regarding the beautiful bronze horses striding over San Marco's portico in permanent triumph. There were perdurable values. Five hundred dollars would see her through four months. Of course she had debts in cities all over Europe and America, but oblivion and lack of expectancy settled whatever pain they'd caused. If she ever got money, she would repay everyone. She did not enjoy this form of making ends meet. Still her work was in the world's interest, despite the world's ignorance of it. She did not regard the money as unfair aggrandizement. It meant a few free breaths to her. Who would begrudge them? Over the marvelous square, beauty itself hovered, a subtle, brilliant companion, honest beyond honesty. She rested her case with it.

That night, contract signed and sent, she added a vinous splurge to her account at Bicci's and talked to her neighbor, Baron von Schöller, an old, semidestitute Viennese playwright who spent part of each spring and autumn in Venice partly for the delicacy of the sun, mostly for the sailors whom he picked up with surprising facility near the docks. The Baron was always amiable with those he didn't need, and once he learned that Nina was as poor as himself he was charming to her. He told her about the empty apartment. "Twenty-two thousand a month and the landlady is amnesiac. When one is in difficulties . . ."

He and Nina understood each other. She put his supper on her account and walked back with him to Campo Santa Maria del Giglio. It was a brisk, gentle night. A half-moon slid in and out of clouds, playing with echo lights in the canals. The Baron lifted a scarf of vines off a palace wall and read in lamplight four lines of Henri de Regnier engraved on a plaque.

"The place has hidden beauties."

"It's why I came," said Nina.

"All your years on our con-tin-ent and you've saved Venice until now. It's hard to believe. There may not be enough time for the obvious beauties, let alone these hidden ones."

The apartment was another beauty, a good room to work and sleep in, a toilet, a shower, a kitchen. Nina promised the baron afternoon teas, something which sustained him in Vienna, but which in Venice he had had to sacrifice to passion. The landlady too proved ideal, a red-haired countess named Lustraferri whose eye wandered from Nina to the baron as if unsure where one began and the other stopped. Either this or another misunderstanding made her suggest that Nina move into the baron's study. "It costs you nothing. In honesty, a gratuity."

"The signorina is a scholar and poet, Contessa. She needs quiet."

The Contessa's arms stretched, suspending the silken, fuchsia sleeves of her dressing gown in welcome to the world of scholarship and poetry. "You choosed perfectly. The most quiet of the cities, and, in honesty, a palazzo that has known poets. Foscolo domiciled here, Lord Byron visited. Now you enrich us," and the arms swung, two large, rough hands plunged from the sleeves, took Nina's and pumped: the transmission of Byron and Foscolo's strength into the palazzo's latest poetic installment.

A week after she'd moved in—Signor Priuli had carried her swollen, old suitcases—Edward, in blue polo coat and white flannel trousers, came up to her as she was checking a book out of the Marciana. "I noticed you were American. I thought maybe we could have a drink together." Sweat-beaded flush mantled his dark face. The large-size panda bears; she knew them. If you watched out for an occasional side-swiping claw, they were good enough company. "Come have tea in my place." She might get a lunch out of it.

What she got instead over her kitchen table was his life story. His lightless, blue-black eyes fixed on his steaming cup, Edward talked and perspired as if talk and sweating flesh away were his life's object. He talked of varieties of love, domestic fatigue, the waste of early promise. He'd wanted to be a theoretical physicist but lacked all requirements except want itself. "I compromised for commerce. And after-hours culture. Forty hours a week peddling perfumed insect killers and vitaminized chicken feed. At night, Spengler and Spinoza. Twelve years of it before it came to me I was flushing my life away. Just last winter. It seems years." He'd left an advertiser's lunch at Batt's on South State Street and was walking the mile back to Noonan's when he passed a crowd watching a couple of men in uniform dragging what looked like a muddy log out of a manhole. "In Chicago it was no log. A fence named Mungelic. The goons had busted his eardrums with fire extinguishers, frozen him in a meat storage locker, thrown him into the sewer. A *Daily News* photographer took his picture. On the train that evening I opened the paper, and there he was. With me looking at him. Pop-eyed, but except for an overcoat of crap, his brother."

"So that did it?" asked Nina, in the burdened pause. She was giving him the attention she'd given confessors all over Europe and the States, an absorptive gift without which, many a month, she would have gone hungry.

"Not that I didn't have good hours, even years. My children. My wife. I love them." Nina withheld the extra breath of relief till his next sentence. "But you become what you do. I was becoming a piece of sewage. Or not me, my life." Nina smiled, a salvageable distinction. "So—" and his long, blue-shirted arm waved toward the French windows, and they both looked out at the cupped, rusty slates of rooftops and the mud-spattered white back of the Fenice—"I came to Europe. Used the kids' college money, sold the house and came."

"Why Europe? I mean I came for the libraries and because it's easier for a girl on her own here."

"It's also easier not to work here. You have a built-in occupation as tourist. Plus what's here. The main thing. I wanted to be around what's lasted. Well, it's been four months. Three in Rome and one here. I haven't caught the fish yet. My money's melting, my wife's—" pause, "chilling, and I'm getting nervous. I've wasted years, ruined one marriage, and—"

It had better be a good lunch, thought Nina.

"Don't want to ruin this one. I can't. And yet—you see, it's part of looking—"

"You've caroused a bit."

"You're a smart cookie, Nina." He touched her cool, short hand; she picked up her tea with it. "I wasn't at all sure. Such a little blue-eyed babe."

"Don't overestimate me."

"I'm too busy on me. Maybe later."

I better not underestimate him. All the better.

"A few excursions. In Rome an untouched beauty at some Catholic finishing school. An American. *Tu connais les types.*" Yes, she knew *les types.* "Sibyl Doubleday. I think her great-grandfather invented baseball. I took her down to Cuma, showed her where she got her other name. My wife found out."

"Another picture in the paper?"

"I keep a journal. Unlocked. Yes, I know. My wife remains mysterious to me. My first one was all too clear. I probably *was* trying to rouse her."

Nina got up. "Maybe this is enough for one session, Edward. Let's have lunch. But don't write it up."

Now in bed, she thought, *love.* Always love. The resort of people who have nothing else. The last phase of materialism. Or was it? She had dissected the subtlest testimony of love's scholars, Ovid, Gottfried, Ciullo, Guido, but *tant cujava saber d'amor, et tant petit en sai.* Nothing she had read matched what

[19]

she had felt in occasional Irish arms in the automobiles outside the half-mile limit of Francis L. Callahan's honorable home on Water Street. Not that she was butch, not that she had hormonic deficiencies, though, worried, she had gone to a doctor at sixteen and gotten a shot of estrogen to see if it would ease her ability to be gratified by the local pawers. It hadn't. There was always something askew, a cleft between desire and perception. Her body, shaped for passion, if she could believe passing hot shots from Providence to Vienna, or, for that matter, the mirror, had felt nothing more than spasms of that erratic crawling which, for fifteen years, she'd known must never become her necessity.

Her poets swilled in the stuff, or so they claimed. Though God knows the Beatrices and Dark Ladies could have been anything at all. The only honest sonnet sequence was the one to "Idea." Those who knew what counted and could not produce it, went for each other, digging for what could really come only from oneself.

Hours she had stood naked in front of mirrors, staring at what had so often been solicited, never given, never really given. Odorless, efficient, rosy instrument, abstractly beautiful. (She'd existed in Berlin posing for painters, all of whom but Hauch had kept their pants zipped.) Only twice had it been called into active service, and then in pity not necessity. First for Hauch, the poor old nut who'd corresponded with Tagore and who paid her fare to Brussels. Then, a couple of years ago, for the red-haired American—George? Charley?—who'd kept her in his room at the Cité Universitaire for two months and whose hunger she'd slaked the last night. There'd almost been something that time. But *Minne?* God, no. His mop bouncing around like the Red Sea in a storm. Clumsy and decent, he'd turned princely, emptied his pockets to get her to Dublin. *E qual soffrisse de starle, a vedere/ diverria nobil cosa, o si morria.* His ennoblement by her sufferance. Who knows?

One covers one's flanks or loses. Her poets might sing that the only gain was loss, the only victory defeat, but that was where she would get off the male train.

Edward. Stitch.

She had all she could manage with her pooch.

chapter 2

I<small>N BED</small>, the blankets to his chin under his beard, Stitch
holds *The Tragic Muse*, but looks instead at his bookmark, a
postcard of Mantegna's Saint Sebastian leaning against the
broken arch, his left foot matched by the marble foot broken
from the Roman temple. Clarity by juxtapose. Andrea could
climb any tower in Europe to examine lettering or capitals.
Henry James climbed to study manners. Henry was at the
beginning of the last chapter of which he himself, Stitch, was
perhaps the last paragraph. Continuity from Greeks, from
Egyptians, Sumeria, China, to James, to Stitch, who remembered James himself in a London drawing room, small, as
wide as high, somehow extricating himself by using, who-was-
it-now, someone like Fanny Assingham as a shield for the
extrication through a door one would not have guessed
could hold him. Or let him loose, anyway. Wonderful eyes.
He had put them as well as he could into the head on the
northwest tier of the island. But not right. Henry's had caught

more light, had a blue-gray glaze he couldn't match in stone. He always had to get force down in the roundabout. Perception watered down. Memory, the part of himself he was losing every day now, which everybody lost, but which he'd not brought himself to lose because, unlike Henry and Andrea, he hadn't cleared up enough, hadn't left enough of what he knew, which as the world and his vanity and his limits went, was something. Though Henry *was* god-awful slow, and he would not finish this book. He didn't want to blur those eyes any more. Henry's. "Hold fast and you keep it; let go, and it's gone. It comes and goes without a watch, and nobody knows its address." *Le Maître*. How many got called that and how many of that many deserved it? Henry, Andrea, Kung. In jail, Perry the rapist called him Perfesser. Because of the beard. Perry wouldn't have known a Donatello from his bars. The only thing he distinguished was what he'd been put behind them for. Do I feel what they call pity for him? Or for myself? I think not. That was the easiest out. Maybe an opening in the north wall, beveled, catching evening light in May and June from the Rememberers group, done in dolomite. He'd have to find the piece. Though he couldn't come close to working it now. Dolomite would have tried him forty years ago. Light. That which mediates between body and spirit. *Lux et Lumen*. The transept at Lincoln. As much of *lux* as he cared to know. Grosseteste. Hermanus Alemanus. He turned the end pages of Henry's *Muse* and thought of what he wanted. He wanted a wall which wasn't wall-like. Everything began as wall, to be bored through, leapt or built over. He didn't want lattice, just the sense of opening, a suggestion it wasn't the same at different times. But

[23]

to order it, to match the difference with the thirty figures in the north group, to clarify. That he couldn't remember how to do. Not even with pictures, not an hour after he looked at them.

Forty years on his island. He should have done as Andrea did, one thing after another; making each count. Instead, it was all thrown away on an island that would go under in fifty years if they didn't dredge the lagoon. Abu Simbel had lasted six hundred times that, and apparently they were going to save it. And Abu Simbel had been finished, recorded. They could do it again. He'd never finished, and for all his notes, for all the critical essays, the interviews and memoirs, Bull's, George's, Pardie's, nobody was going to turn thought into stone. And he worked no longer. Slept and shoveled in food, and excreted, painfully, read, but like a sieve, dressed himself, with help, thought, but with difficulty. The subject for other people's memoirs. Friends who had thoughts of their own and so missed his. Bull, Pardie, L.O., Yves, Perosa. And the enemies who wrote the quickest and easiest.

He'd always known that ninety per cent of what was known about anybody was baloney. Enemies wrote and bystanders. He could see an account forming in the fathead at Nina's. Dazzled by celebrity, a groveler, a witness of events, a newspaper reader with protective covering of names and tags. A Jew of course, in essence at any rate. A secondhand dealer. Not knowledge but opinion. Yes, he'd be written up splendidly there. Though why not? He deserved the worst. And God knows what that mattered. For fifty years they'd been writing about him and he couldn't think of a single one of the thousands of stories which had seemed to him accurate in feeling or detail. He'd once spent a month checking standard biographies of three sculptors: all stewed in minor errors, destroyed. Yet Frederick on hunting with birds was authority after seven hundred years. Aristotle on fish lasted two thousand. Accuracy. So he'd had to spend hours in archives around Europe and the States, in Cairo, in Delhi, working with the sources of what became part of Sant' Ilario, the Isola di Stitch they called it now. Maybe more useful before he'd cluttered it up.

Lucia spent hours each day trying to heat up his memory with memories, but he could barely nod to what had been. He'd never liked to live much in what he'd done more than a week ago. What he'd thought, planned, worked out, yes. Now, each month brought a death—and the few were fewer. He could do nothing. Except eat. He no longer had strength to cut stone, memory to spell out what he would like others to cut. And what he left, his sixty years' work, was so oblique, so dark. When he'd wanted above all ascent into light, enlightenment, order, spelled out as the Egyptians spelled it out, as the Indians did against Hindu bunk, as Dante and Homer and old Bach and Kung and François Arouet had spelled it out, the human order which mirrored the cosmos, the divine ordering. Years and years, what were they now if he'd left only disorder, hints, scattered notes? Waste. And self-inflicted as much as anything. Despite years of warning against the Corruptors, the bedeviled innocents, the poison-beetles who loved nothing but their own stink and the death of those who didn't help them make it.

Himself. The self that was now, after the fifty he'd made and shed, the two or three he'd left maybe a little clearer than the rest on Sant' Ilario.

When he'd first come to Venice with Grandmother, age

[25]

eleven, he'd sat on the lions in the Piazzetta and triangulated the moon with the angel of the Campanile and his shadow. The old Campanile. Not too many left who'd seen that. And the next time he'd come it was in wreckage, two days after it had fallen, Bastille Day, 1902, *el paron de casa*, though in Venetian miraculousness, the fall had hurt nothing but a corner of the Libreria. He remembered the Marangona sticking intact out of the pile, a mute hippopotamus, the only bell which still rang. Then about 1912 there was the Campanile again. The measurements had been taken, it was indestructible while Europe had memory. While it was Europe. Now fifty more years, four hundred and fifty for it. Though there had been a tower there since Pietro Tribuno, a thousand and fifty years ago, and God knows what Roman ancestor of that. No, campaniles were from the sixth century.

He'd never been up to see the city from it. A mistake. He might still take the elevator up. His island was supposed to be visible. In the air age sculpture should calculate from above. Leonardo said sculpture depended on overhead light. On nature, therefore inferior. Perhaps. Leonardo was against any collaborator. *Contra Conjugium.* It would be worthwhile, though God knows what could be done if his stuff were a shambles from that height. *Sub specie deorum.* Ant work.

And whom he'd seen here, such girls, the first one, nameless now, faceless, but the body remembered, pliant under hands, and holding the light. Lit spheres, breasts, rump, met in Campo Margherita, a Parmigiana, visiting the rubble, oh it had not been easy to find speech for her, she had, he supposed, found it for him.

He should have stayed here through the war. A mistake. He

would have been safe. No. That was not remakable. He'd done what was in him to do. His portion. There was still rightness there, if the world could be right. There was always winter, despite guys like Bucky who wanted to take it out of life, install permanent atmospheric gentility. Climate was a desideratum. You couldn't bring beauty to birth in the Arctic. It was hard enough with babies, a much tougher if less distinguished principle of order.

Yet the ranting, the persuasion, the talking into the toilet, years and years when he should have been cutting his stone, leaving something clear. But who knew that anything would be left if that paralytic had kept on paralyzing whatever lived in the country. What was one to do in a world of three billion semithinking animals, bunched into sties, squealing for swill, what was one to do short of extermination but take over from them? It was no longer going to be possible to have what had been had off and on since Egypt, since Sumer, since Harappa, the clear line, the beautiful object, the fair price for the well-made good, bread that was wheat and wine from true grapes, a cuisine out of the mind. All that was over and Andrea was over and St. Apollinaire and old Bach and San Zeno and Sosthenes Three. There'd be other things. Not for him. His island would sink when they didn't dredge the lagoons. The whole city would sink. Bradysism. No. Stupidity. Egoism. Vanity. Where he was expert. He had tried and tried, but neither love nor pain nor hate nor pleasure, nothing but beauty, and that was brief, could put it down.

He was lucky he was here, alive, a live pig, for there was almost nothing else. But sloth. Greed and sloth. The refining doctors of the church mapped out human viciousness. If they'd spent more time on heaven than each other, he would sit in their pews. Some of them he'd sit with anyway. Occam and Grosseteste and dear Ambrose. God knows they were men, minds, in or out of their doctrines.

He was lucky to be here even slothful and greedy and vain, for there were years when he thought he'd never see the Campanile again, or Ca'd'Oro, the Miracoli, the Carpaccios, the Giudecca. On the stone walls he'd faced for a hundred and twenty-one months, he'd seen them now and then, though he'd had to take down the Canaletto and the John Bellini or the tears would come, and he could not stop. If his mind alone did the work, then the tears were few or kept in his eyes. Why was that? One cried in the body. Now his body was blunted, and he had to lay it so flat no breeze would add weight to it. His mind, incapable of fixing that which for fifty years anyway he'd fixed so clearly there was nothing he could not find that he had once known, or could not find with the aid of a telephone or letter. Evil communication rots everything. Yes, that was not from the Oriental side of wisdom. Clarity, the clear word, the well-cut stone, the adjustment to light, the clear mind, the ordered file, the, the . . .

❦ chapter 3

For Thanksgiving, the Gunther children stayed home from school, Nina was invited, and all gathered around a twenty-pound turkey roasted in a Campo Marte trattoria and carried down the fondamenta by Brose, embarrassed by the culinary opulence before his ragged companions. Cressida had contrived a stuffing, and only cranberries and sweet potatoes defected from their annual menu.

It was Nina's first turkey in a decade, and this was enough to keynote the celebration: home, the gathering of fellow countrymen amidst alien corn.

If the dinner cheered Nina, it depressed Edward. As he hacked away at the great bird, it struck him that he stood very close to where he'd stood the last time he'd carved a turkey. For two weeks, Cressida had been at him to make plans, write agencies, to get himself and them set for next year. The dwindling bank account gnawed at her. While he was making out Adrienne's alimony check two Thursdays before, Cressida had said, "What do pickpockets do when pockets are empty?" Though for months now she'd been strangely sympathetic to this woman she'd never seen.

Edward told her to mind her pots, he'd take care of himself and the children; she'd never lacked bread, nor for that matter, cake. Look how they'd made it to Italy with three children, including a year-old baby. They lived in a palace on lawfully-gotten gains. His. They were part of international life. How many of the world's specimens could say as much? How many of Noonan's other secretaries had queened it in Venetian palaces?

But over the tender leaves of turkey breast, he ached with the unfinished, the barely begun. Cut down like the fattened bird before he'd come to something. And to what end? What great maw was giving thanks over his damages?

"Why so gloomy, Daddy?" Cammie, his chief observer, black eyes bright on his face, his pretty dark little girl, heavy with premonitions of puberty.

He could only shake his head, try a small smile, hack at a wing joint.

"Daddy misses lunch in town." Cressida, blue-green eyes snapping, disregarding Nina's presence.

Quentin woke up in the back room, and Edward went in to change him. In the darkened room, he kissed the baby's delicate cheeks and hair, sang to him as he powdered his bottom:

> Ooh look at Quentie
> He's heaven-sentie
> Ooh he's a sweetie
> From head to feetie.

What love he felt for this baby. He loved the others terribly, but Quentin purely. How long would it last? Till the will fattened, challenged, evaded, connived. "Quentin, my darling," and he carried him down the hall and into the study where the others waited for Cressida to bring cherry tarts. Even in the noon sun the air was sharp here. In a week they'd have to close it off and Edward could no longer lie under the great baroque angels affixed to the wall or break his reading to look out the window at the Ducal Palace when the vaporetti swished by on the half-hour. Now he lay down on a green divan, Quentin on his chest. Nina played Christmas songs on the Steinway, Brose and Cammie sang, Cressida knitted. Venetian still life.

Quentin's *bambinaia,* Signora Lydia, a pyramidal mount of devotion, called at the window. "Qveentie." Quentin squealed, crawled, disappeared. Half an hour later Nina went off to the library, Cammie and Brose out to fish with weighted strings off the fondamenta.

In the cold room, lines of silence crackled. Cressida's head was down, not so much toward her needles, as away from Edward's look. Fair, golden-haired, fine-browed, her skin was slightly mottled by an odd scarlet, as if allergic to their being alone. Edward wanted to ease the strain, but could not. What was there to say? Cressida was so expert at chilling peace offerings. And perhaps he at offering provocations. At night, their amorous sessions were constrained by the narrow beds of the rented palace—lined up head to foot—and a cold unaccustomed silence as if they separately pursued different if interdependent missions.

The sun up, each domestic event became either occasion for argument or a barely avoided one.

Winter in the fields. If only it were but seasonal. They both hoped this. Neither would say it. Spring must come of itself.

[31]

STITCH

That night they slept poorly, separately, and, the next morning, the mail complicated their animosity. The Talman Federal Savings passbook arrived showing a balance of $4,830. Edward, in pajamas and sweater, came into the kitchen to join Cressida for his morning's coffee and bread fixed with the soggy English peanut butter he made do in Venice. The passbook lay open, weighted with a knife whose point was at the figure.

"Why the knife?"

"I don't know where it's gone, but it's gone too fast for my nerves."

"The coffee's cold."

"It's hot till nine o'clock."

"Till nine, the kids are cruising around. I don't relax enough at night to take that before coffee."

"Your troubles."

"There's two thousand more in the First National. That's why the passbook's here. I withdrew it for the checking account. We could live a whole year on it. In fact two, if we'd live low."

Cressida raised a hand—where would it go? he flinched—and slapped the table. "Do you realize the only low item in our budget is my shopping? Do you know how much we spend on food here? Not much more than Lydia. Can you show me one other American in Venice who shops in Campo Marte? No."

"I wasn't talking about your shopping, but as long as you dragged it up, you shop in Campo Marte to show off in front of these Giudecchini. 'Look at me, the rich American lady, down here with you rubes.' But all you're doing is paying more and getting less. You're so damn concerned not to seem any better than Olga and Lydia. Showing off for them like you used to for me. You turn the whole shopping business into a reverse potlatch."

Slap on the table. "You spend more in one of your little lunches than I do all day. You spend more having coffee in a week than I have on clothing since I've been in Europe. You think you're the American Crown Prince come over here to loaf your life away and ours to boot. You and your self-examinations and reflections and studies or whatever other camouflage you're emitting these days. Why don't you get off your fattening rump and do something before you drag the whole lot of us with you?"

Edward went to his room and dressed, a little earlier and more rapidly than usual, shaved, and without looking at Cressida again, left the house.

He took the vaporetto over to Venice and walked to Nina's.

"*Chi è?*" The mutt was at his feet, yapping.

"*Io, io,*" and leaped up the stairs, made his way in and kissed her lengthily on the lips.

"*Cosa ti ga?* I'm not receiving." She was in wool pajamas. He had not realized how small she was, how worn. "Didn't get to sleep till three. It was that turkey. It sat on me like divine wrath. I read old letters, a thing I don't let myself do every night."

"Nina, Nina, it's sympathy I'm looking for, and have no way of deserving. Not even self-pity here. Just anger. I meant to bring a bottle."

"There's half of that Vecchia Romagna you bought Monday. We can put that away. What is it, ten o'clock?"

"Quarter of."

"We'll not be bound by the clock. Wait a minute," and she went into the kitchen for the bottle and glasses, poured double shots and brought them in. "Want some tea? Crackers? That's the limit."

"Got a good mind to make you my heir and drop into a canal."

"Here's to you. How much is left?"

"Couple of thousand. Enough to float us months."

"I'd last ten years on it. Two anyway. You'd better stop buying me lunch though. Cressida biting your ear?"

"Poor thing has nothing better to do."

"It's a nice ear," said Nina.

Edward laid his glass on the coffee table and leaned over her. The mutt, yapping, jumped on him. "Put that hound in the bathroom."

"I will not."

"You're more nervous than I am."

"For some reason, I am. Believe it or not, I am a pure thing. Not undriven, but pure."

"You're not a bad-looking little thing," and he raised her pajama top. "You're something." He put his left hand on her breasts, surprisingly full.

"I think not, sugar," said Nina, and pulled down her pajamas. "No offense. But I think not."

"I'm no nookie-chaser, Nina."

"Other people's property," said Nina, which she could say and had said in six languages to waves of pinchers, intruders, rapists who saw in her isolation the almost-institutional establishment for their endowments. Nor was she going to bandage marital wounds. As a matter of fact, she would probably be a terrible disappointment to him, and this could lead to what was not necessary or desirable, a breakup.

Though the hell with the lunches. There was Cecco Angiolieri on his father to do this morning. "Come on. Walk to the Marciana with me."

"It's too cold to walk."

"Suggest an alternative."

He did.

"I don't have much, Edward. Don't make me lose it."

She undressed in front of him, confusing reward with provocation. Still in overcoat, a deer-brown Loden he'd bought in the Rialto, he was on her, embracing her stomach, kissing her breasts. She shoved his head away. "My fault, sorry, sorry, please don't," and went into the bathroom, calling out more apology.

Edward felt the humiliation not of rejection but of his desire, and this fused with the sense of uselessness which weighed on his mind, even as the desire left his body. The fusion took the form of a monster headache which sent tears onto his face. When Nina came out in a red skirt and yellow sweater, he had to avert his head. She came round, saw the tears, took his head in her arms and kissed his eyes. Neither spoke. Neither understood the other, nor attempted to.

Then they left, she with briefcase, he with nothing. At the standup bar by the Ponte delle Ostreghe, they took coffee *macchiato* and creamed egg-and-artichoke sandwiches. Edward left her at the Marciana and took the *circolare* boat for Murano, a two-hour round trip in a warm cabin which disguised his aimlessness.

❧ chapter 4

Wrapped, encaped, hatted, scarfed, booted against the piked December cold, Stitch looked more flagship than pirate. Up and down the Riva, bridge to bridge, he wheeled and tacked about waiting for Nina. Five minutes late, and he five minutes early. The walk had put a smoky rose amongst the reticulations of the cheek, crystal blazes in the green eyes. Nina, spotting him before he'd seen or acknowledged her, felt a rare timorousness, then went into his line of movement and aroused him to his habitual courtliness. She was hatless, had on a thick blue coat—Aggie's refurbished hand-me-down—and a red scarf studded with blue arrowheads that, with the cold, brought her face to more point than it had indoors. Stitch lit up at the sight of her, held her hand in his for greeting, and inclined his fedora toward the motoscafo which twice a week made a stop at Sant' Ilario, l'isola di Stitch. She got to the ticket window first, but he gloved her away, removed from layers of cape and coat a wrinkled green purse of felt, withdrew coins for two round trips, and bustled her along the planks and into an inside seat. As the ropes were unwound from the black stanchions, he said the first of the two things he was to say on board, "I haven't been out in two years." He had suggested they go at their last night's tea, "The cold will insure isolation." Now his fingers drummed his knees, his eyes were on the lagoon; he'd lost her. It was a fifty-minute trip with one stop at the asylum and another at the tubercular institute. There he muttered the second thing, "We're all either loony or *krank* out here in the lagoon."

Nina was not entirely easy about the expedition. An interview in Rome's *Daily American* had Venice's rich American artist, Mrs. Fogleman, calling the island "Stitch's fraudulent folly." Who knew?

Only she and Stitch got off at the island. "It's never overcrowded." There seemed to be nothing but dirt and a hill, a dirt path, a fulvous hill. Stitch had leapt off the boat to the path and moved more quickly up the hill than she'd yet seen him move. He stood at the top, outlined in the iron air like a giant condor. Nina followed, head bent under the wind, stomach gripped by a notion that maybe, just maybe this was it, that there really was nothing but stones and a hill.

"There it is," taking her arm, pointing the cane with his other.

Eighty or ninety yards squared from water edge to water edge, five hundred, maybe a thousand colors firing up from blocks, spheres, triangles, polygons, thousands of colored shapes, some surfacing as people, horses, turtles, plants, silos, villas. Yet, at first sight, it was as if the elements of formal creation were waiting there for tankers to carry them back for incorporation in the real city still visible over the water.

[37]

STITCH

In the frosty wind, Nina burned, perspired, tears in her eyes, partly now from the sinking feeling that what was here was decorative chaos, the cemetery of a brilliant ambition.

His hand was at her elbow, guiding her down, first to an intricate amalgamation of twenty stone textures which, as Nina looked at it, became a horse's neck and muzzle.

It was a marvel, a dazzling surprise. She could not look away from it. Each segment was a complex of stone linked to the next by flaring whorls. "Believe it or not," he said softly, "it's Rome."

"The horse?"

He patted the muzzle. "Glad you see that. There's a little more to it. It starts down there, see, the yellow-brown block. That's the tufo, the *ruber et niger tophus* of Vitruvius. They dug it from the Palatine and Capitoline, 600 B.C. It's a bad weatherer, so it stands here, weathering. Later—farther, here—" pointing with his cane, "they coat it with stucco. That bit there, next to the greenish band, that's *capellaccio*. Volcanic, a conglomerate of sand and ash. From the left bank." His cane touched a spar of golden stone. "San Pietro in Montorio, *Monte d'Oro,* because there was a yellow beach up on the Gianicolo. Now you get the city walls. *Lapis Albanus, peperino,* the brown, studded with black scoriae. Harder stuff. Then layers of *travertino.* Mostly ornamental, till the Empire. The Colosseum. First century B.C. It goes for bucking up small pressures. Here," and the cane distinguished a baby vault, "it spreads in a swell, waves for the naval power they lacked and which saved the Eastern Empire." Stitch walked behind the pointing cane tracing a creamy line. He spoke as always, quietly, precisely. "You've got to lay travertine horizontally. The crystal won't take stress. That's why the Rostra cracked. But it weathers. Pure carbonate washes out in running water and calcines in fire. It's all in Vitruvio, what your hands and eyes can't tell you." He walked up a yard. "Here's Augustus. *Marmor Lunense.* Carrara. Suetonius says he 'found Rome brick and left it marble.' He didn't mean brick. The brick's just facing, a layer of paint. Not quite. In the Pantheon, twenty feet of concrete for the vault, six inches of brick. Which helped center the mass during solidification. The horse's neckline, see the tiny bricks? Baked 'em myself. Underneath, concrete, a few hunks of marble and brick fragments bedded in cement mortar, *opus albanum.*" Talking to her, to himself, to the stones. "There are the four white and nine colored marbles, limestone's children as limestone is water's. You see what it means for—" and he waved the cane back across the undulant skin of lagoon toward the Venetian towers. "Out of the sea on the sea's shoulders, the shag crystals of sea salt in the very stones. I've got all the marbles but one right here, and the absentee I get obliquely. With tricks, angles, and a bit of steel. To show you can get something if you want it hard enough. And then to connect with my time, with Sullivan. See, over there," and the cane pointed to a thrust of steel banked into what seemed a cave, but was, when Nina followed him over, a jagged Pantheon with some of the colors and textures of the Roman history wall. "You see? If you stand here, you see the steel in the wall, and then the Gandharan stupa which'll help you look at the skyscraping. The concept's there, Nina. It's there. What sculpture is to space, architecture is to place. Architecture is the *fils,* not the *père.* But it could be clearer, clearer. Couldn't it, Nina? The forms? Everything? But some of it, some of it can be seen. The Golden Age stuff, from Indus Valley to the Mayan. Over there." Ten yards through God knows what mazy tumuli were two marvelous coarse-grained trunks in intercourse, the female up, one delicate hand on the male organ, the other caressing her lover's cheek, small figures, isolated in the forest of stone, and somehow afloat.

"Yes. That's clearly something else." Still, for now, she preferred the equine wall.

There were heads of Stitch himself, some cubist, some partial, many with women, one of whom was surely a young Lucia, all different in posture, look, age, stone. "I come in and out of it, depending what I'm thinking, or what's happening to me, or where I fit in at the time I'm working. And there's Bully, Jacob, Georges, Charley Ives, Lloyd, Buckie. And Ezra, Igor, Arnold, that red-speckled feldspar there like a trumpeting throat. Polygons are polyphony, lines monophony, and tribe rites to go with them. See? They're to blaze and fuse."

Wandering, by leg and eye, Nina began to find much more that was familiar to her: there was a sort of shorthand group of Donatello Davids arranged not as in the Bargello but as sequential studies of weakness becoming strength. There were two semicubist Michelangelo Depositions, one like the one in Florence, the other like that in the Castello Sforzesca, here set up facing each other so that the roughed-out inachievement of the second seemed a rebuke to the completed, personality-charged assurance of the first. There was a declension of Egyptian heads, from the oblique formality of early dynasties to the full-lipped irony and passion of the middle, down into Greekified versions which crossed with Greek versions of Egyptian formalism and led to another plane, a shelf of green-veined marble with a Phidian Athena in high relief on a temple slab.

There were versions of quattrocento low reliefs, Neolithic animals, the tiny Venus from Willendorf. This without apparent alteration, "because," said Stitch at her elbow, "for the ritual stumblers into truth you need only the fact itself. It's the great founders you have to go at obliquely, to unleash the old power." A history of sculptural peaks, though "when I don't know something, Polynesia or the Eskimo, I omit it. Or if everyone trumpets it, like Chartres, there's no need for it here."

There was a kind of Campo Santo with fifteen or twenty figural interments, some vaguely musical, some judiciary, one in which Nina recognized the broken-nosed power of Michelangelo tangled into a marble rebuke of its own power. The shapes seemed to be straining toward and failing to arrive at human form. Next to the Michelangelo—or anti-Michelangelo —was a sheer hole, a void that somehow, amidst the great whirl of stone and metal, took an oddly prominent place. Nina started to inquire about it, but Stitch passed over it fiercely, deliberately. He took off the hat, his white hair studded like porphyry, swung his stick in the air, and, raising his other arm, presented it. "Nina, here it is. Here's the old buzzard's droppings. Lifting, bearing, embracing, fucking, gathering, worshiping, hoeing. See the wall hoeing."

"I do," said Nina. "I do." A basalt stretch from which arched a bladed strut. "It's more than I'd have believed."

"There is something, yes," but as if puzzled, disappointed, arms down, hat on. "Not as it was meant. And wrong, here, there, though God knows I thought everything that was here was right. But something."

He walked to the hilltop, his back to the great labor. Nina followed. It had been three hours since they'd met at the Riva.

She was extraordinarily elated amidst this inorganic garden of high sanity.

He went on down the hill toward the little pier. When she caught up to him, he was sitting on the railing, eyes on the motoscafo cutting the lagoon on its return from Alberoni.

✿ chapter 5

T<small>HE WORST, THE COLDEST WINTER EVER.</small> In '24 when
he and Lucia first came to this house, the canals froze. You
could walk from the Giudecca to San Michele. In '88 the ice
was supposedly two feet thick; six years before he'd come. For
an old man, for a man whose kidneys and memory and nerves
shivered with weakness, this ice was more than enough. Ice
would suffice, as that provincial put it. Caina. Giudecca. Judas,
Cassius, Brutus, ice in their noses, their eyeballs. Lucia rose
twice a night to stoke the stove. He guessed the readings within
two degrees centigrade: his bones registered more precisely. His
own head icy, nostrils, toes, ankles, groin, festered gonads, spine
base. Down, down flat under the piled blankets, eyes just over
them, all he could risk to the daggered winter. What was the
human use? Cosmic hatred. He'd been too sure of its order, if
not its benevolence. So easy when your head was so full of
stuff you never worried about saving anything. The truth was
rock hard, water clear. Your world the best that had been said

and done, the best alive who'd said and done it. London, Paris, Rome, Venice. Where things were done, said, redone. Like Henry, he'd had to leave the provinces. Now his body made him a provincial. Worse than the cell. Awash. Head a dark gallery. No more shows. Seventy years of surety. Ice would blacken the island, draw the string veins out of the stone, twist the light. He hadn't planned for such cold. Let alone the rising lagoon.

And what of it? He'd be meat before long. Why not? There'd been no passion, hardly memory of it since the medicine men picked at his gut strings. Slave devotion, a few lines, a few bars, flickers.

Breakfast, hours yet. Wake Lucia. Not even window light. The plastic window sack stifled light as well as cold. Lucia. Old dear. What's the good of propping the ruin? He should have checked out in jail. Yet he'd gotten Newton done since. And Mencius.

Cold. The tester. Sits in bones. Cold. A man of the South judged by the North. In part. He'd turned Italian. There was no heroism in Italy. Everything at once clear and suspect. This dear boot. Northerners tuned to spooks, fire shadows. Enamored of danger. Yet skeptic. Salted. Salt sharpens pain. Yet fools suffer too. Another thing learned too late. An Italianate villain. Punished by the all-or-nothing North.

Working on the island. September '44. Working a week or ten days on . . . on Pānini, Aldus, Caxton, the Preservers. The first good period in two years. The rest of the time had been guff. The rant that consumed him for six years. *Stitch on Power. Stitch on State Control. Stitch on the Perversion of American Politics. The Yeses and Nos of Fascism. Soldi e Soldati. Ac-*

comodatevi. Mussolini contro la Guerra. Speeches in Padova, Milano, Mantova, Catania, Messina, Napoli, Bari, Puglia, Ancona. In '36 the trip to the States, ramming it down Bankhead, Borah, Nye. "Wish we were all as high-minded, Professor Stitch." Isolated, maybe turned fanatic by the chill. Turned fanatic, though never totally out of mind. There were essential distinctions. There were relations of passion and there were relations of money. Until they were sorted out, one had no right to work on islands. No utility, no fructification, the state pegged on death. Sixty billion a year. And matched by the Russians. Accumulating ultimates. Mortared by innocent stupidity. Stones, themselves innocent, piled, made prisons. A great wall of lies. Zaharoff. DuPont. Schneider. Krupp. The crew-cut killers lying to themselves. No. Not fanatic. But no more. Too late. And not all clear. Not sure. Agassiz was sure of boundaries between living and non, sure of immutability of species. But wrong. A *mensch* after his heart, yet had to be tested, as he had tested the good Humboldt.

He'd been on the island. Late September, sapphire and ermine, the fish smell on the breeze. Working. The motorboat, an underthought of surprise, though now and then one heard them, patrols, police, no one else had fuel. Six or seven of them. Revolvers at the waist, rifles, the chicken-turd *marron* of uniforms. Two had good faces, cheekbones, china-gray eyes. The officer, toothy, cheeky, small, a feather voice.

"You Thaddeus Stitch?"

"As ever."

He'd written he'd be available for interrogation; he knew a few things. Two or three months before, he'd started to hitch to Florence, meet the army. Then Luigi wrote the Partisans were gunning for him. They'd shot up the house in Girgenti. His stuff, the world's stuff, finished. Pardie's drawings. The Padovani Codex—he'd copied only five of the motets. The bust of Sophie. So he waited in Venice. There was a time when it looked bad here. Partigiani had passed through Mestre shooting up people. A few incidents on the Giudecca. He'd moved in with Perosa.

"I'm ready to testify."

Not their readiness. A little nigger, sweet-faced, had gotten out handcuffs. The chinless one laughed them off.

Over to Piazzale Roma and a jeep to Verona. They would not let him call Lucia. In the Palazzo del Consiglio, the statues like a tiara, Catullus, Vitruvius, Young Pliny, who else? Marched under *Pro summa fide, sumus amor,* 1592. While the white Dante statue watched. Perhaps he'd be shot in the Piazza under those blind eyes. Which would have been that. Suppose *he* had died at Campaldino.

His own fault. Six years. Was he worth the Codex? Pardie's drawings? *Non lo credo.* A piece of infected meat. Months later, Muss and La Petacci, upside down in the service station. Under Dante's eyes. Under Western. Jacob's bust of Conrad. The gush of bronze, lava off the skull, eyes like antra in the backcountry.

The cell in Verona, next to Perry. And he had sketched the whole of the war section there under Perry's yells and the wop killer, and the rat feet, and the shit bowl. And they would not let him see Lucia or Catherine, and he had no word. In the courtyard, said things to the wind. The cold in his bones, his head aching without remission.

Then blank. Or, what he could not face, rips in the blank.

Mind squeezed, drop by drop, out of his head. New York, the courthouse, five blocks from where he'd lived with Aunt Jen, the park, the horse cars, the old Square. Henry's Square. And the three thousand days. Wilde had broken under his. And at times . . .

Dawn noises, boats, crates slid on fondamenta, cats, talk. Lucia up, helps, sleep, coffee, boiled eggs, prosciutto crudo, sleep, lunch in bed, Lucia, "Nina coming for tea. Are you up to it?" Nod. Yes. The good eyes, the peace. Nothing coming in. But peace. The bell. Cover foot, sit up. Hold to it . . .

2

The fire in the raised brick fireplace warmed and shadowed the three of them. Sitting up in the long double bed, Stitch's head was in the room's center, marked by the ceiling's peak line. He was covered, feet to waist, by a brown wool blanket. His green knit sweater rose from waist to beard. By the bed, a long table with books, sketches, water glasses, a few small figures, bronze and marble, eyeglasses. Shadows rose and fell behind him on the wall. His face worked by the years in a way art had never caught, a marvelous production. Terraces, canals, rivulets, hillocks of forehead and cheek were hardly connected with the undamaged features, the distant, gleaming, verdigris eyes, scarce scrub of eyelash, pyramidal clump of nose, the lips showing barely through the peppered hair of mustache and beard.

He must surely know some of the effect, thought Nina, but did not belittle it nor him for contriving it. He lived by the eye as she by the ear.

[47]

Miss Fry sat or left or carried in or passed around. Today, she was little needed to fill the silence, for Stitch talked. "I came on the tailwind of the romancers. Self-expression for general edification. Having looked at a few things, I could not subscribe. I fell in with African work. At Apollinaire's. He got it from old Frobenius in Frankfurt. An Ashanti mother carried the *Akua 'ba* so she'd bear a long-necked child. Thin-hammered circle, nose cylinder, two metal ruffles for eyebrows, a spiral neck, the Greek cross of body on a base, a foot or so high. Once found, no need to vary. Jacob was doing the British Medical Association pieces then. Vomit poured on 'em. You find less of 'em today than the Parthenon frieze, which our neighbor Morosini went after in more direct fashion. I was hit hard by the juxtapose. There you had a society demanding beautiful work in the natural course of life, here one which sat cross-legged to throttle it."

"Don't functions fuse in simple societies?" Nina, mostly to keep Stitch talking. "Stonemasons and carpenters are their artists. You can tell in the work, its geometry. The reproduceable simplicity. Airplane designers are the equivalent. They're artists with recognized social functions. They speak of perfect aerodynamic forms."

"Yes," said Stitch, slowly, but though quiet, roused. "The tear shape. You have something. Worringer said line was abstract, alien. Maybe the West works better with broken forms. Harder to duplicate. I don't want to claim more for the Africans than for Quercia or the Pisani. And the West has anonymous, function-full work that's unmatchable. St. Trofîmes, San Vitale. It's not till Michelangelo that you get the terrible egoism. Then the deluge. Since, we've compensated for social loss with grotesquery. The ego, contriving its own ambiance. I should be pleased so numb a skull," tapping it, not softly, "managed as much as it has."

"A pretty good head," said Nina. "And very fine to contemplate."

Laugh from Miss Fry. "He was always something splendid to look at. I remember you cavorting in the caves at Gaeta. Those —what were they?—Swedish girls. Staring: Balder *retrouvé.*"

He shook his head once, unacknowledging the memory: the eyes narrowed, the lips widened under the hair. Silence sank in the room. Fire dominated it. Crackling and wild shadows from two large logs. "I'd better get more logs," said Miss Fry, and to Nina's "Let me," she indicated Stitch with her hand as if to say, "You're his present. Stay here," and went downstairs. Nina felt but the slightest pressure. After a minute, Stitch talked again, so quietly and suddenly it gave her the odd feeling that the silence had condensed under the intermittent rub of the fire shadows. "One senses the loss of nature's grip. Fields, forests, change of season. Maybe Venice prepares you for the gray world. It's got so little green, it seems seasonless till you know it." And without perceptible transition, "Old buildings came from nature: arches from hills, thrust and lintel from tree and sky. The new forms are getting ready for space. The forms I've loved are natural, earthly. Not void, fire-blast, hollows, form beyond eyes' reach. Rocks upon lumps." Another pauseless shift. "Three hundred and forty million in the U.S. by 2000. Six billion on earth. Rockets go up for fun in '62; they'll colonize in '80. No more lives like Jefferson's. Or mine. Or yours. Natural lives. Spacious. In nature. The best were farmers then. 'The greatest service which can be rendered to any country is to add a useful plant to its culture, especially a bread grain: next in value to bread is oil.' That's Jeff. Brought in olive trees from France, upland rice from Africa. Not much of a farmer. Flat busted at my age. For all his efficiency studies. But he stuck it. Knew what counted. And wanted to preserve it. End entail, end mortmain, end primogeniture, educate, keep the church off the state's back, the state off the individual's. Jefferson to James. Antityranny. That's what I was after. Maybe Jeff yielded a bit, some new book on it. They say I did too. May have. Have been wronger than righter. Who knows? There may even be some farmer-king making interstarry odysseys. An interstellar Homer. I doubt it. It's the end of Europe. My stuff won't even bubble going down. As if it matters. Though it does matter. If there are no survivors, no rememberers."

Stitch's arm swung, snapped over to the table, his hand grabbed something and held it out to her. "Here, Nina, you take it," and with a green flash of smile under the white scrub, "before it goes down." His arm waited, raised, until she went over and took from his two fingers a bronze centaur, wild, puzzled, a beautiful straining little thing.

"Oh, Mr. Stitch."

She put it to her lips, then picked up his hand where it had fallen on the blanket, and kissed it. Too full of joy and sweetness to look at him, she went to the fire. The topmost log was breaking up amidst small roars of spark and splinter. It broke to a hundred colored bubbles, vermilion, purple, orange. New shadows swept the room. The silence came back. With it, Nina felt a long warmth swell inside her body. For this old magician, who'd so finely gifted her, she felt great love.

❧ chapter 6

THE STUDENTS OF the *Istituto dei Catecumeni* were collecting money for the lepers. The funds were to be sent to Padova the Friday before Christmas accompanied by the best school compositions on the theme of Charity. For two weeks before Christmas, Brose and Cammie's energy and cash were mobilized by collection and composition. Treats were sacrificed, tasks were requested, money was borrowed against forthcoming birthdays. The evening before submission, Edward, who had donated nothing to the cause—"my charities are private"—agreed to play Twenty-one against Brose's collection, "to show him God doesn't approve of good works or they wouldn't be needed in the first place."

The game began after the children wrote out their final drafts, florid Italian implorations of grace and beatitude which came automatically to their pens after three months of classes inundated by piety and sermonizing. They played on Edward's bed, his usual after-supper retreat in the Venetian winter.

Brose and Edward were equally competitive, and though they

had drawn closer together in their European isolation than they'd ever been—for the first time Edward regarded the eleven-year-old boy as a friend to whom he sometimes spilled his latest insights into world affairs and doubts about his own— there was an active baiting of each other which frequently culminated in arguments, shouting, accusation, and blows. After Brose's tears on such occasions, Edward could face his idiocy objectively, and then love for his sturdy little son would soften his fierce heart and he would offer apologies Brose was sometimes too proud to accept.

Now he and Cammie knelt by the bed where Edward lay under the covers and dealt the cards onto a ledge of sheet. Each hand was accompanied by invocations to deity: "Dear God," said Cammie, "give us an ace for the *lebbrosi*." Edward would pull threes to eights, top them with queens and sweeping up Brose's fifty lire respond with, "If God cared about *lebbrosi,* he wouldn't have started them out that way."

Brose's 4,000 lire went down to 900. The children held a council debating a halt while they still had something for the fund. Cammie wanted Brose to stop, but sporting blood flooded caution and charity.

Brose began winning. In an hour, he was back to 4,000 lire, and to Edward's growing fury, got to 4,500. Cammie said, "Quit now, Brose."

"Can't until the deal passes over," said Edward.

Brose won again. Edward played recklessly, hoping to throw the boy's game off.

The count went up to 5,200 lire before Edward took the deal on a twenty-one he'd bet only fifty lire on. Coldly, he said, "You want to quit?"

Cammie pulled at Brose, whose vision of tomorrow's presentation to the *lebbrosi* returned in force. "I guess so."

"Don't guess. Yes or no?"

"Yes."

Edward threw the cards on the floor. "Out."

Brose and Cammie left while leaving was safe. Minutes later Edward heard them telling Cressida of the triumph.

He threw off the blankets, ran into the kitchen, and walloped Brose on the backside. "Some trustworthy little son of a bitch you are," and amidst tears and shouts from Brose, Cressida and Cammie, he got back beneath the blankets.

The next day Cammie announced that they had collected five times more money than anyone else in the school, and besides, Brose's composition had been selected to go to Padova. Although Edward discerned a link between the triumphs, he was proud that his son's work was so honored. "Of course those Venetian kids have trouble with Italian grammar, but still it's remarkable." He apologized for his behavior, and gave Brose and Cammie a thousand lire apiece to buy family Christmas presents. "Or treats," he allowed, but in a way which let them know what the proper choice was.

2

For Christmas, Venice was in high polish, chill, brilliant, ice-colored. Gussied-up by family seamstresses and tailors, Venetians marched in *grande panache* from church to café. For two weeks pairs of shepherds had hopped through the calli, skirling goatskin bagpipes and wooden flutes, collecting against Christmas Eve returns to their mountains; friars in white, black and red canvassed door to door; postmen, milkmen, daily purveyors of all sorts made their semiannual extractions, and now paraded with brilliantined Gianfrancos and curlicued Graziellas upon the gorgeous stage of their city.

The Gunthers were in the Piazza by 10:30. Cressida and Cammie assisted at High Mass in San Marco, the three male Gunthers strolled—Quentin on leash in his elastic harness—through people and pigeons, aglow in the aftermath of strenuous gift-opening under not the annual evergreen but the sooty face of the stove, Warm Morning.

Huge in his deer-brown Loden and Christmas-green Borsalino, Edward bestowed bows on neighbors, storekeepers, fellow library readers. *"Bon 'atale, 'ofessore,"* from Signor Bicci, coated and scarfed to his rocket head which was capped by the cousin of Edward's hat. *"Buon giorno, amori,"* to Brose and Quentin from the nurse who administered their typhoid booster shots, a demure *"Buon giorno, Dottore"* for unboosted Edward.

Their third march round, Edward spotted Stitch, Miss Fry, and another woman coming in under the Correr archways. Farsighted, he discerned from fifty yards the Stitchian features of the young woman. He started forward, then felt he could not meet, brood to brood: Stitch had once called the family "the seedbed of tyranny." (Edward had read two biographies of him in the Marciana.) He turned the boys around and went off to the bar under the clock tower for hot chocolates.

Brose drank his at the door, assigned to watch the emergent communicants, Quentin distributed his over Edward's new tie, one of the ill-made Italian silks that had but charm of surface. The result prevented more walking *en famille*. They returned in a domestic funk from which only Nina's appearance for Christmas dinner relieved them.

The dinner—featuring their second McGowan turkey—was a grand success. Brose and Cammie had used their lire from Edward to get Nina and Charley presents (Nina's a bead necklace and earrings, Charley's a rubber bone); Nina had made the Gunthers a fine ink sketch of the Piazza.

After lunch they opened the study to Warm Morning's scrappy bestowals, and there they received the three after-dinner guests, all Bicci-acquaintances: Oskar, an ex-Croatian, ex-landowner who now ran a pensione on the Zattere; Jaska, a Dutch painter who churned out six Venetian scenes a week for the tourists, and her lover, Fabio, a corpulent, gentle lawyer who, like not a few members of his crowded profession, busied himself in extra-legal activities.

Cressida cooked a gallon of red wine, mulled it with cloves and cinnamon, made the children milkshakes, and candled a large chocolate rum cake. All fell to. Steaming wine plucked the air's sting.

There had been some talk of asking Stitch and Miss Fry out, but Edward felt that all action on that front had best be initiated by them. As it turned out, Nina said, their daughter had come up from Agrigento for a few days, and Edward, Cressida, and she herself were invited over for tea to meet her.

This invitation played a part in Edward's own good spirits. To be included on Christmas Day in a Stitch family affair was an investiture of cultural nobility. It made up for not being invited along to Sant' Ilario. With wine, cake, his family, the rented, old palace, his earned trappings, Edward yielded to euphoria. And when Jaska, large, soft, blonde, blunt-featured, played up to him, the children, and his *belissssima chassa,* and when he heard himself conversing with Fabio and Oskar in his high-wire Italian about Fanfani and Saragat, he bloomed with self-confidence. A citizen of the world, a joiner of hands across the sea, a cementer of NATO and the Western ecumene. Nina did no talking. Politics was not her dish of tea. Nor was Jaska. She disliked her manner of life and her looks. She was extraordinarily clumsy, whereas Cressida, though large, was a kind of matronly Atalanta. Beside their bulk, Nina felt like a water rat. Physically. As for their respective lovers, she felt she could have had them with sugar for breakfast. With one whistle. Fabio was a gentleman, but his popped black eyes had shivered meaningfully at her. And poor Edward was trying even when he thought he was holding back. She wasn't alone in seeing it. When she was around there was a tightness in Cressida. Although Nina never doubted her own innocence, she did everything possible to ease Cressida of discomfort, pumped her about the problems of shopping, heating, clothing, caring for the kids, made her tasks seem herculean, her triumphs miracles.

Cressida's tension however, was not a reaction to Nina, but to her realization that she felt literally numb toward Edward. It was astonishing. Even when she'd been furious with him, she could feel love underneath the fury. Now there was nothing left. Edward played a role in the family, one which could be played by anyone, but which he played by virtue of the past alone. When she'd come out of San Marco this morning and found him standing there with Quentin and Brose, his shirt and tie gored with chocolate, her heart had nearly contracted out of her body. That this filthy, shiftless, self-satisfied bum should be in charge of her children was outrageous. All the way back home, all during the preparations for *his* Christmas dinner with *his* friends, she thought, I've got to leave him.

But how? She was helpless. Here in Europe with three children, no money of her own, her mother thousands of miles away, and not much help there. There was nothing to do. It would have to be lived out. At least till next year. And what about then, what about getting to next year? He'd made no plans, had nowhere to go, not a hovel. The money leaked out day by day as he took himself off to feasts at Bicci's, opened the house to his tribe of friends, bought hundred-dollar overcoats for himself. And the outings with his girls, which she'd poached from the idiotic journal he'd kept in Rome. The delicate Sibyl. That had begun it, she supposed, but now she didn't care about his whoring around. All the better; he'd leave her alone.

So she sat, golden and helpful, passing wine, cutting chocolate cake, checking on the kids, smiling under the barrage of Italian, waiting till they would all go, Edward and Nina to their tryst with Stitch, Oskar to whatever he took himself off to, the corpulent lovers to bed.

3

Nina and Edward headed toward Calle Ramigero through the crowds coming back from the football game with Mantova at Sant' Elena. The sun dropped gold off the Salute; night hung in the lagoon. Canal waters were aflare with color, the air with café riot. "Couldn't call this a dead burg now," said Edward. His heart bubbled with excitement. Through the loud calli and over the packed little bridges he guided Nina, one arm through hers, the other stiff for clearance, a huge rectangle of brown beside a firm little foot soldier in a red cape. Striding immense in the thin streets, he felt toward Venice like a boy with a model train set.

On the fondamenta noise and lights fell away, and in the twenty-foot calle with the six small houses their steps clattered.

The door was opened by the youngish woman Edward had seen that morning. A fine, solid, fresh-cheeked face, with a high curved forehead, large, light-blue eyes, hair the color of Cressida's pulled back in a fat knot. "Miss Callahan. Mr. Gunther," looking up at them, with, thought Edward, surprise at his bulk "I would know you both from the nice things said about you." Had he made so good an impression in his twenty minutes with Stitch? His nervousness fell away.

They went into the first-floor room which was filled with great-backed wicker chairs and hooks from which Stitch's capes and odd hats dangled. "It's awfully nice of you to come. Merry Christmas." They reciprocated. "They're upstairs. Why don't you go up? I'll follow with tea." She called out, "Mother. Father. Miss Callahan and Mr. Gunther are coming up. I'll take your coats." Edward laid his Loden over her arms. Nina kept her cape, and he followed it upstairs.

On the second floor, Miss Fry, in tweed skirt and gray sweater, stood by the staircase, hand out, smiling. "How good to see you." All shook hands warmly, Stitch, standing by an armchair, silently. He was in a checked jacket, slippers, soft gray shirt and sweater. As usual, he looked somewhat hastily put together, and, because he was underweight, both large and small at once.

Edward felt immense beside him. Indeed, he felt that the little room itself was stretched by his bulk.

"You've met Catherine. Good. She hasn't been up in a year.

In fact, hasn't been in any town but Girgenti, which is hardly a metropolis. Although Venice must not seem like one to you, Mr. Gunther."

Edward told her that it felt so this evening, but then to cover a renewal of nervousness he poured out talk of Chicago, its museums, its crime, sports mania and beauty, and was advocating some Stitch sculpture to replace Meštrović's Indians when Catherine came up the stairs sideways with a tray. He leaped up, took the tray, shoved some books off the table putting it there, stepped on her feet as he bent for them, apologized, straightened, just missed the chandelier, dashed in to take the first cup poured and brought it to Stitch, who, expressionless, waved it with a wrist snap over to Nina. He passed all the cups, then handed round the plate of cookies, again coming first to Stitch, who again waved him to Nina.

All sat back, Edward in a butterfly chair where he sank like a stranded whale.

Catherine von Goedlingen had paid her first visit to the States two years ago. She was, she said, enchanted by the ease and grandeur of life there. The lack of trouble in banks and libraries, the general trustworthiness. It was a splendid contrast to Europe. She'd lived entirely in Sicily and Austria. "My husband is attached to the University of Innsbruck. Yet, if there hadn't been so many bridges burned, one would think of re-claiming—moving. I am officially, in passport, and I guess in heart, American."

"Best to be American and live in Europe," said Edward. "The other way round and the baby goes out with the bath."

"What does that nice expression mean?" she asked her mother.

"You must ask Mr. Gunther."

"Ahh," said Edward. "I pass," and he waved toward Stitch, who sat hunched in his sports jacket, staring at his daughter and Nina across the room.

Catherine laughed and said, "I'll never learn now." Edward explained it, and then wondered that English was not her first language, she spoke it so well.

"How good of you. My range is very small. Isn't it?" she asked her mother.

Stitch said, "You have lacked the opportunities of Mr. Gunther."

Edward did not measure the time between this and Catherine von Goedlingen's reply, which was, "It's clear Mr. Gunther has merited all he enjoys," but he knew something unpleasant had happened.

Stitch stared straight ahead. In the canvas depths of the great chair, Edward managed to say, "I have been lucky."

Stitch did not look at him, but said, "The luck is part of a system. Mr. Gunther's talk is more schematic than haphazard. He ensures his success by inventing fifty-eight per cent of what he says. He quickly takes over where others give way. He invents what he needs to fill gaps."

Stranded in his own bulk below the level of everyone else, Edward felt the heat of their attention. His eyes were pressed by rising blood, his face ached. Above him, he saw but half of Stitch's face, which, oddly, wore an amused look. He croaked out a response. "I'm sorry you feel this way. I guess much of what I say in company is—well, frivolous. Though I can't recall anything I said that's sheer fiction." And then, to accommodate whatever Stitch was feeling, for he didn't want an explosion, he added, "Perhaps my training hasn't prepared me to distinguish fiction from fact."

Stitch nodded two or three times, his beard splayed on the sweater under his jacket. "An effective answer. I particularly admire the way the voice falls away. It's good to know we're watching theater. We don't have to confuse it with anything real."

Edward, realizing that the Stitch ladies were not going to come to his rescue this time said, trembling, "I'm sorry my answer appears theatrical. I don't intend it for effect," and he shook his head and faded off, crumpled. Is this madness? Antisemitism? Fascism? Or was the old fellow explaining his life to his daughter who must have had some mighty bad times while he was in prison? No, there was more. Chicago Semite *Venitien?* Not that. That was too easy.

Stitch had sunk back into silence, a signal for Catherine and her mother to speak at once, loudly. Was Nina getting enough heat in her apartment? Wasn't Venice terrible now? Where did she buy coal?

For ten minutes they went on, then Nina said she had to go. "Good-by," she said coldly to Stitch. "I'm glad to have seen you," and went downstairs followed by Catherine and Miss Fry.

Edward wondered if he should even say good-by, decided it was his duty as guest and gentleman. This would be the last he would see of Stitch. Yes, the reports were right. He was a broken Fascist. He turned to him—the old man was still staring at the floor—and said. "Good-by. I'm sorry I annoyed you. You're partly right about me," and held out his hand.

Stitch raised his old lion's head, looked into Edward's eyes, then brought both his hands over Edward's and drew him down. Edward bent over nearly double. The hands held him. "Wrong, wrong, wrong," said Stitch. "Eighty-seven per cent wrong. I've never been able to recognize benevolence." The green eyes shone from the depth under the white scrub brows.

Edward, hand held tight, felt his back cracking. He went down on one knee before the old man's worn-out face, trembling. "Oh," he said. "No. Not so. If you've been wrong, how about others?" The raddled head shook back and forth. "Yes," said Edward with sudden authority. "There are probably mistakes. But what you leave is there, clear and right."

"Notes," from the barely moving lips. "Scattered notes."

"No," said Edward. He patted Stitch's hand with his free one. "No. The Tate bronzes. The Rememberer's shelf. They're there. All the way." The head denied, the hands held tight. For help? For companionship? "You wrote the bigger the bite, the harder to—"

"How about once on the wrong road, it's too far to return. I can't remember. You don't know what not remembering means." Headshaking, trembling, hands tight. "Only sure thing is nothing's sure. I know nothing. I used to think there was something to know. This," the eyes blinked green, in, out, "doesn't exist. No Europe any more. The idea of Europe's gone. The last rememberer, crawling out of the wreckage. And I can't. No bonds—the past," and the voice stopped on the trembling lips.

Edward felt tears coming, fought them, tried to speak, felt his voice break, could but shake his own head, "If, if, if only," and stopped. He drew his hand from Stitch's. The old man looked straight into his eyes. Appeal? Message? Edward touched the checked shoulder for good-by and went downstairs in a trance.

[62]

4

"I would have walked right out." Nina, sitting over Bicci's ossobuco. "You know he was winking at me while he was chewing you out, don't you?"

"No, I certainly do not." All right. Maybe there had been a little exhibition as well as true feelings. "Even so, I wouldn't have walked out. I'm not a hero with an eighty-year-old man. Let alone a great man. Even if he is a little off his nut."

"Off his nut, hell. He was just raking you over the coals."

"He had it in his head I was monopolizing things. Talk, the room, playing host in his house. It was offensive. He was right. What do you want him to do? Maybe he was showing off a bit for you and the daughter. Showing he could still take on the punks. You were looking particularly elegant. Don't think that doesn't count with a man. Even an old futzer like Stitch." But he didn't like to say this. Why demean?

Nina's cape was softly military, richly red, the sort in which a princess would review troops. With the red of her cheeks, she seemed nature's own contribution to the season. "You're just evading. I'd never speak to him again."

"You missed what counted for me." He'd told her about Stitch's appeal on the way to Bicci's.

"Baloney."

"Baloney to you, baby. It was as shaking a thing as ever happened to me," and he drove into his ossobuco and would not look at the merry, pug face. Nina reached across and patted his hand.

"Friends?"

"Naturally," and he bent down and kissed her hand, leaving a broken sauce ring below the knuckles. It would take him some time to work out what had happened. It wasn't simple. Stitch's antipathy was not simple. Simplicity would have made his confession—which was what really counted—impossible. Edward had not been just Anyman then, as he had not just been Ikey Bleistein at the beginning.

Oskar sat at their table.

"Old Stitch just gave the business to poor Edward here."

Edward burned red as a yelling baby. "Nonsense. Why in hell can't you get anything right, Nina? How in Christ do you think you're ever going to be a decent poet if you can't even report a situation correctly?" and he told Oskar his version.

In telling, he found it oddly blurred. Trying to make it clear, he amplified the benevolence of the second part, hastened over the sharpness of the first.

Oskar was interested, but though lesser transactions made up the stuff of his days, the scene was no more nor less than one of them, a bit more evidence of the world's melancholy grain. "People doesn't comprehend each other. A old man. People age, they get quick-temper. It don't mean a great deal. Vhat you eating, the ossobuco? *È buono? Allora, Bicci, dammi mezzo ossobuco, niente pasta, nient' altro. Ho mangiato troppo a mezzogiorno.*"

Edward got up. He had to think through what Stitch had told him. So much of what had happened to him had washed off, unpondered, barely felt. He'd never held on to what mattered. Holding on was what made a man a Stitch. The man who felt the hardest, the one who didn't run away from what he felt, who knew what happened to himself, was the man for whom everything counted, to whom nothing could be accidental and thus catastrophic. The rest was remembering, and, if you were an artist, getting it down. But remembering exactly came first. Stitch couldn't, which was the death in his face.

"Will you excuse me?" He signaled Bicci to put Nina's dinner on his check and walked out.

Nina shrugged, surprised, a little put out. "I've offended the poor jerk. What a klutz I am. You can't tell a dog his bone's unfit for a man. Does no good at all."

5

The night was quiet, windless. Edward's feet ached, humped in shoes he'd paid a bargain price for in the Rialto. He unlaced them, and then walked slowly through the empty calli, eyes on the half-moon, chest filling with cold air. In Campo San Barnaba, he stood at a bar and drank two shot glasses of grappa, then went on through calli and campi past the Frari into Campo San Polo. The lopped moon hung over the great square; the rimming palaces gathered its pallor on their fronts.

Across the way, detaching itself from palatial stone, something moved, came forward. A woman. She swayed. Drunk. All of a sudden she leaped, hands stretched, heels clapping below her coat, legs spreading. A nut. She pirouetted into the center of the campo. Under lamp-and-moonlight Edward recognized her. Adela. An old whore who showed up everywhere, cadging money. A week before, she'd approached Edward showing him a Mickey Mouse watch on her wrist, telling him it was a family heirloom, the lawyer had just found it after a year's search, she would not let it out of her hands for a fortune, did he have a hundred lire, the bank was closed and she had to get to Milano for a conference with the lawyer, consulting the watch whose hands were painted on half-past four. She had a long, grizzled fox-face. Her eyes were gray and wandered, her hair lay under a filthy beret on which collapsed a broken plume. Tonight, Christmas night, she was performing for herself.

Edward left the shadows and came up to her. "*Buona sera,* Adela." She turned easily, hauteur agleam on her hairy muzzle. "*Buon Natale,* Adela."

Her response to this was a graceful elevation of her coated arms from waist to plume. "You're a fine dancer, Adela." Where did she go after the dance? Adela croaked something. What did you say, Adela?"

The long muddy face pointed to the moon, but she was after meatier custom. He took four hundred-lire coins from his pocket and handed them to her. "Not tonight, Adela," and walked toward the western end of the campo.

The coins hit him in the back. Adela shrieked, "Bugger, shit-chewer, dog-fucker." The campo shivered with the clanking riot. People ran out of the bars and to the palace windows.

Edward ran for the turn-off, went up the first side calle and leaned against a wall, heart leaping, face streaming. "What a nut I am, what a nut." He'd approached her in fellowship. And what happened? Imagine pumping that grizzled flesh. What a finish to Christmas.

He went into a bar for grappa, then walked to the Piazza and got the 10:29 vaporetto for the Giudecca. There he insured himself with a final glass in the *Tabacchi,* then walked, a little shakily, down the fondamenta and into the courtyard.

The water fountain splashed away. The moon took a beating in its basin. Up at the kitchen window Cressida sat at a table, coffee cup at her mouth, eyes on a book. Her Christmas—from her mother—green wool sweater came to her chin. Her head was touched by the kitchen light; the precise features shone through a golden fog.

"Oh, Cress," said Edward.

He walked up the steps past a bannister of sleeping cats and tapped on the window. She looked up wide-eyed, not quite frightened. He smiled, waved, did not wait for her to react beyond surprise, but opened the door and walked around the heaving stove and into the kitchen.

"You startled me," her head back to her book.

Oh no, Cress. Don't look away. He wanted to say something about Christmas, about their life, about reform. But didn't. She would respond with something about the warmed-over spaghetti she and the children had eaten for their Christmas night supper while he caroused. No. He could tell her of Stitch, Adela, of what he was trying to understand, of walking through the streets. He'd come into the kitchen with pity, then love; it was but a few minutes from this to more love, and from there to—who knows?—renewal.

She looked up questioningly, "You all right?" and he hesitated, it was an opening, but it was formal, something to break his stare.

"Why not?"

"That's true. Why ever not?"

He stood filling the doorway, his Loden a weight on him. What to say? Where to start?

"You should've come."

STITCH

She did not look up from the book.

His spine began to glitter with pain. Miserable bitch. Adela.
Nina. And this one. "Good night."

A grunt from the fog.

❦ chapter 7

J ASKA AND FABIO gave a New Year's Eve party in
their long, smoky apartment in the Palazzo Da Mosta-Correr
in Campo Santa Maria Formosa. Edward, a party-lover, could
hardly wait. In Venice, parties had been few and miserable.
Although their apparent *raison d'être* was display, their manifest executor was parsimony. An American-born countess had
given the first one on an October Sunday in her apartment in
the Palazzo Balbi: a few antique, threadbare Venetian nobles
of second and third rank zooming for the single plate of
cucumber and cheese sandwiches, and a clutch of foreigners,
McGowan the consul, a Fulbright professor at Ca' Foscari, a
Swiss publisher's representative, a few art historians, the
Gunthers, and Mrs. Fogleman, the white-haired, softly malig-
nant, expatriate painter. These spent most of their energy trying
to locate a uniformed *cameriere* who'd poured one round of
gluey sherry and disappeared. "Perhaps they're saving it for
the next party," said Edward to Cressida. "Or there's another

one down the Canal," said Cressida. They'd been having one
of their better days together.

Fabio and Jaska's party was filled with talk, pretty women,
good whiskey, food, and a barrage of Venetian characters:
Avvocato Vidale, a squat old Venetian Jew, local chronicler,
and gossip, Civita, a wall-eyed multimillionaire consul general
of three Latin-American countries, a clumsy breast-squeezer and
loud-voiced propositioner, and Dottore Scarpa with his mistress
of forty years, and her husband. "No absentees but Adela and
Bicci," said Nina, who appeared cloaked in Charley's rug, his
rubber bone occasionally in her teeth.

For it was an optional costume party. There were great-
bellied eighteenth-century dresses and masks, togaed ancients,
cowboys, grizzly bears, hootchie-kootchie dancers, Pinocchios.

Edward had come alone. "Cressida has a cold, and Signora
Lydia couldn't baby-sit for us." The latter was fabrication, the
former as true as not. He hadn't known Cressida wasn't coming
—he hardly ever knew her intentions any more—had only assumed she would. At nine, she still sat in the kitchen mending
Brose's pants. He said, "You'd better start changing. Probably
be a good idea to be there at 10:30. Lydia doesn't like to stay
too late. We can catch the 9:56."

"I don't feel much like going. I don't know these people."

"What about Lydia? She'll be coming down here."

"I'll give her some coffee. She'll be glad to get back to her
television. You go on. You enjoy these things more without me
anyway."

"I enjoy everything without you, because there's nothing to
enjoy with you." And stopped, though he wanted to say it
wasn't the way he wanted it.

"I know. You better go on."

There was nothing to fight against. Well, it was better than bloodletting.

He met Lydia on the way and told her to go back, the signora wasn't going, no, she was just a little tired, nothing else, *Salute e Buon Anno.*

He was uncostumed, untuxedoed. Nina reproached him. "Get with it." She was feeling chipper: her manuscript was in the mails for Oklahoma, and she was primed for the big work. She wanted it begun in this Ecumenical Year, and so had worked up an opening line from the *Purgatorio* an hour before putting Charley's white shag rug over her old green evening dress: "The sails upon this ship attend the wind." Launched toward the New Year, a chick in dog's rug, propped with two self-gratulatory shots of Vecchia Romagna, she was ready for action. More booze at the party sent her roaring around, a formidable confrontation.

Her first victim was Civita. She put a hand on each of his soft arms—though the rug, leashed round her front, would have shielded her from his lunges—and drummed him with English, a language he scarcely understood, "Why don't you unshell some of that gold you got in there?" arm detached to poke his stomach bowl. "Whyn't you ever get out and do something for the arts, you know you got more money than Rothschild? Why are you such a dirty little chaser, squeezer, lush?" Her eyes triangled with anger, her breath rich in Fabio's whiskey.

"What after, what after? *Porque? Che vuol da me, signorina?* Maybe think I am someone else. Consul, Uruguay, Paraguay, Colombia."

"Stay where you are, you greaseball rat. Smellpot. Come

across. Why are you such a tightpants? Pay for your pinches. Miserable *hombrero*." Though puzzled, Civita went for this and in a roll of Spanish begged her to remember her place, who she was, what ladies did, what gentlemen would think, what Uruguay and America, or England, or wherever she came from, would do if there were an unfortunate brawl in a foreign city. "Honor, honor, my dear senorita. If you are indisposed, let me go for assistance. Lie down a *momentito*," and spotting McGowan leaning over Mrs. Fogleman, called, "McGowan, mister. *Vien qua, per piacere*. One of your country ladies. Look. Help," which raised from the hard gray globes behind the consular spectacles a gleam of morcnic lust. McGowan moved across the room and aimed his hand for Nina's pinioning right arm. Edward crossed over to intercept him and took her off. "I'll handle this, Ambassador." He moved her to Fabio's study where the whiskey was. "What, but *what* in God's name are you trying to do?"

"I'm having fun. *Laisse-moi*," and she went up on tiptoes, pecked at his lips and slipped back into the crowd, this time for Avvocato Vidale, who, from a slender armchair, addressed two lawyers and a blonde contessa. Nina's Yankee Italian speared in. "Dear Avvocato, what is the source of your remorseless tedium?"

The broad face gaped.

"Ah, you can't explain it, *cher mafioso*. The talent is mysterious. That's the way with great gifts."

"What makes you wish to hurt, *figlia mia*?"

"I wait for your response, *avvocato mio*."

"I've heard you were a good girl, a gifted girl. Are you ill?"

"*Che pazzeria, signorina*," from the contessa.

Avvocato Vidale said, "The Anglo-Saxons have the habit of declaring themselves on New Year's Eve," squinting at Nina so but a line of iris showed. "Speak up, child. Declare yourself. Have you need of a good stiff one? Are you restless? I wish I could help myself, but lots here will oblige."

Nina spun, the white shag sweeping the avvocato's face, moved off, and called back, "Too easy, Avvocato. Don't give me that old screw talk. You've bored Venice to death for ninety-nine years." And faded toward Mrs. Fogleman, who, too late, was dodging away. "Cheapskate," hissed Nina. "Penny-grubber. Anal gorger. I know ya." The shag drove the old woman toward a glittering snow daub of San Trovaso. "What's losing the tickle like? Or do you lose it, you ancient old tooth?"

"Filthy little drunk you are. Cheap little pervert. Get away, disgusting thing. Go away, or I'll have something done about you."

Irish up, Nina closed in, face inches off the frightened woman's. McGowan gazed in stuporous excitement. "What's your contribution to the modern state? Name it. That you don't wear pants? Big thrill for the pigeons. You're as sexy as this rug," shaken out. "Artist? You wouldn't know Dürer from your greasy twot," and spun away, looking for more grist.

She found Edward, who grabbed her up, rug and all, and carried her down a dark hall two bedrooms away, put her down on the bed and sat beside her. "What in hell has triggered this?"

Nina lay back, nostrils flaring, subsiding. Small violet blotch marks showed in her cheeks. Her eyes were dilated, her throat muscles worked. Edward was thinking he'd better get a doctor when suddenly her arms came out of the white shag and pulled

[73]

him down on her breasts. Her heart boomed in his ears. Her knees drew up and tightened at his rib cage.

"I'm drunk, Eddy. I'm drunk. I'm stupid drunk. Ughhhh. Give me, give me a kiss," and lifted his head and kissed him from her depths. Never, never had she felt this force.

Edward rocked with it. He started to break off, but something had happened. What the hell. "Let me, let me get the door, Neen. Let me up," but she would not, her arms metallic, knees flexing, legs holding him. Too much. Wildness. He got himself open, reached in under the white shag and green dress, pulled her pants down and off, and pushing up, met her. There, with the party noise crackling down the dark hall, Edward knew his first real ease in weeks and Nina an untimed storm which, as it ebbed, brought her to a calm so rich it palpably transmuted itself into sleep.

After a minute of repose on her body, Edward righted the pants under the dress, resettled himself and left, closing the door. He walked back to the party, dodging Nina's victims till he felt calm enough to tell them she was sleeping off an alcoholic indisposition but wished him to make her apologies.

At 2:30, as the partygoers began leaving, Edward woke her. She looked up, unsmiling. "I hope to God there'll be no consequences." She got up and went around the apartment saying good-by, apologizing to Jaska and Fabio for "twitting the characters."

Walking home with her, Edward wondered if she could possibly have forgotten she'd had intercourse with him. Until she said, "I'm almost at my period. I suppose there's little chance."

"We were lucky in lots of ways. That's the wildest that's ever happened to me, Nina. You may be a vestal three hundred sixty-four days a year, but, my God, what a New Year's Eve performer."

A kind of yak in her white shag, she was up on the hump of a bridge before he'd even realized she'd left his side. There she spun around, her eyes blue fury. Her mouth opened, something came out, not words or spittle, but something between. Her hands went to her head, and she tapped it, then pointed a finger at Edward. You, it meant. "You piece of junk."

His thick Loden, the drink, fear, physical exhaustion clogged his impulse toward her. He managed, "Nina," but by "Listen" she was down the other side. He leaned on the bridge's cold balustrade, eyes on the canal's black water flecked with orange moonlight. What have I done, Nina? Have I brought you down to me? Is it what that old futzer saw in me? Is all my thinking just for this? Breaking Cress? Breaking you? Did I leave Chicago just for this?

The vaporetto was full of celebrants, drunk, loud. Edward stood alone outside in the chill watching the light flares strung out in the lagoon to guide ships. What a joy-boy. Cargo delivered, ashes hauled. Oh, Nina. Isn't your furnace cleaned out too? Why resent it?

How would she know anything if she didn't know she was capable of this? He'd been of use to her. She'd see it.

Ten minutes later he hit his hard bed, his head three feet from Cressida's soles through two end slabs of oak.

2

Every night now Cressida went to sleep exhausted, the dishes put away, the stove fed for the night, the indispensable ironing

[75]

ironed, and as soon as her eyes watered over a Penguin novel
or her brain watered at what her eyes brought to it. Still,
anxiety shook her and she woke every few hours, made her
way down the corridor to the kitchen, and there, as often as not,
was shocked by two flaming circles spooked on the dark
windows—one of the staircase cats, its life probably as settled
in permanent disturbance as her own. Sometimes she opened
the freezing study and stared across the water at the pins of
light stuck into sleeping Venice.

This New Year's Eve-Day, her third insomniac bout occurred
at 5 A.M. and she decided to let Quentin's matutinal demands
break on Edward's snoring head—she'd heard him rumble in
at three or so, a rolling sack of self-content. She piled on two
sweaters over long underwear, put on wool stockings, a shirt,
her all-occasions blue coat and walked out on the fondamenta.

Starless, moonless, the air sharp almost to heat in her nostrils,
she breathed it in deep relief, feeling it displace her troubles.
She walked past the Zitelle, past the single track on which the
delivery men hauled fuel, past the fermata, the Redentore, the
moored tankers, up and down the bridges. A vaporetto swished
toward the fermata, lighting up in front of her: the conductor,
the ticket stamper, and one passenger, an old woman. On past
the prison gardens and Princess Aspasia's, the traghetto and
Sant' Eufemia. There was talk coming from a canal to her left,
men in a fishing boat, and she walked near enough to see by a
lantern hung on the pier. Three men were sorting crabs,
fingering the bellies, throwing them into pails. A boy trapped
eels under the struts, stuffing those he caught into a canvas sack. The light lit half a face, a flopped rain hat, a hand,

smoking breath. She couldn't follow much of what they were saying, prices and some Giudeccan talk, *cosa ti ga, q'ranta franchi, sche, muoia-ti,* a soft speech, lisping, remote, intimate in this peeling backwater. A woman came over with a net and negotiated for *sento franchi*'s worth of the stuff, enough for a family *zuppa di pesce,* twenty dollars a plate in the States. A wedge of comfort. Maybe they can live on their thousand lire a day. Lydia came up here two mornings a week. It could be managed. Edward. Eel. It was the New Year. Decision time. She would have to begin operations, shake the fog out of her head.

It was Friday; maybe she should buy fish. Mother and Grandmother feared Catholics but ate fish on Friday. Edward also. Part of his self-rejection? It was somehow stranger to her now that she'd married a Jew than it was when she was deciding. If anything, it had been a positive factor, a piquant, defiant appeal.

The 162 pounds of her mother had come near splitting. "Ay Je-ew? Cres-si-da Mag-ru-der. Ay Je-ew. Are yew absolutely out of your my-und?" Her mother's own southernness, out of Missouri via Illinois's Egypt, showed only under stress. "What dew yew think your grandmother'd dew. She would spuh-lit."

Cressida's grandmother, six feet of remote parrot, somehow held together, splinters ready for ripping, and offered her a "brand-new secondhand car" if she would give "that young foreigner" up. After all, at the Magruder Genealogical Conference in Rome, Georgia, Dr. Tippen Magruder had traced the line back to Noah. The Magruders had never in their history been mixed up with boys from the West Side of Chicago.

This in front of the cracked mirror in the bed-sitting room where husbandless mother and husbandless daughter pooled recollections. Secondhand cars? Going to the Loop was the month's extravagance.

She hardly dared derange them with her love of the mild but exciting young man. Thin—at that time—dark, young, Edward was so courteous and kind and handsome. Ay-rab, Je-ew, or passing Negro, if her few charms could do the trick, he would be hers.

He seemed really something then, smiled all the time, darted around like a big bird, full of light remarks and answers for things. Everyone could see that even Mr. Noonan thought he was smart. She'd been wowed by him from the minute he showed up. And, after a while, he so dazzled her mother and grandmother that they began thinking of him as a foreign branch of the Magruders, a royal branch which would raise the depleted fortune of the locals.

She didn't learn about Adrienne till two weeks before they married.

She should have thought then about whatever defect had let him conceal such a thing from a fiancée. What was too hard he ran from. Sure, he was the best copywriter at Noonan's, he even suffered in his work, and he was good to her, but woe betide them all when things were the least bit astray. Years and years she'd taken his outbursts, his depressions, his posturing self-contempt. He'd seen that, perhaps had married her for that. Oh, he wouldn't admit it, might even have been unconscious of it. As he was of his fawning before the university swells of Hyde Park, soaking up whatever rot came out of their mouths while he frowned her into silence if she dared question one of their sacred texts. She'd read a heck of a lot by then, more than most of their wives who spoke without pause or sense half the time, or sat back and acted as their husband's auditoriums.

What had happened? Natural attrition? Age? Constricting life? Two lines which had never been parallel diverging more and more? Or maybe it was the institution itself, good for a decade, the rest sufferance?

She turned back now, empty-handed. On the rim of the lagoon the sun edged up. In front of her, towers, churches, boats reared up out of dawn swirls. "You've given me lots of trouble, *bella mia*," she said to the town. She felt a little like the escaped prisoner whom they caught last week in ten minutes waiting for the vaporetto to the mainland.

A prison made of jokes, a town of water, a wife of habits. No, she couldn't stay here, couldn't stay anywhere with him. Forty more years of attrition. What was the point?

She hadn't been in the house a minute before Quentin unfurled his morning cry. Once again Edward would sleep undisturbed.

3

Nina restored Charley's rug and bone and lay on the bed, head at the pillow, crying. She would not let Charley leap up to her. No one. Nothing. What had she done? Everything she respected, twisted. Under the shag she had been worse than Charley, drunk, bestial, stupid, lax, vile. Every disgusting impulse acted on. And finally, that, that response to her whatever-it-was, which God would not be wrong at all to turn into a life that would then and there stop what she had for a dozen years aimed at, prepared for, sacrificed to. To have had her own quick way, knocking over whoever stood there. Cressida, whose hurt she'd seen, in whose home she'd had happy hours. She wasn't sure of marriage rights, wasn't sure how much Cressida cared to have Edward with her, but who was she to bulldoze her? Bypassing institutions sacred to God and man. This was what Francis L. could never condone. The tricks of one's own skin were nothing to this.

And yet it had been as if determined.

No. She could have stopped. Any time. Civita, Vidale, Fogleman, the booze, Edward. Any time. The wind that filled those sails had come from her own insides. Nina was Aeolus. Nina was the bag. Nina the wind. And Nina's would be the wreck. Dearest Mary. No. No rights. Let it come down.

Charley wept on his disgraced rug. Also right. Unto the seventh generation.

Her hand below to her eased flesh. No. No ease. She must stew. She must not beg off. She must not know any ease but confession, which must not be ease.

When her mother reported the sexual laxity of high school girls to her father, he looked up from the paper, nose—her own fat nose—flared. "What concern can that be to our daughters?" Which was it. There were no restrictions in addition to their knowledge.

Yet the human condition was not angelic. Did this matter? No.

She'd been a piece of filth, a slut, a coward.

Humanity.

The Church allowed that. But for someone who'd trained

and trained, who had the leisure and means to study virtue, the circumstance for its easy practice.

Let the tremblers get mobilized by the vortex. Not the poet, trained in abstinence to be the witness of their wrecks.

Let the child come as her rebuke.

4

That morning, in confession at seven, taking communion at eight, Nina issued fresher, but met what she regarded as retribution. Charley, instead of waiting for her as always by the entrance to the house, was not there. Nor was he in Campo Santa Maria del Giglio. The gondoliers at the traghetto had not seen him. The bellboys at the Gritti had not seen him. She walked to the Piazza, but it was a holiday, and neither vendors nor shoeshine men were there. She walked to Campo San Stefano. Adela was leaning against the church, hand out, head down on her right shoulder, eyes closed in assumption of sanctity. "Adela, have you seen Charley? My dog?"

The fox-face stirred. The eyes stayed shut. "Sì, signorina. He run over the Accademia." Nina followed her finger, crossed the bridge, and went through the calli, calling, "Charley, Charley."

She walked two hours. There was no sign of him. And no one else she asked, restaurant people, familiar faces, had seen as much of him as Adela.

At the Frari, she felt the flow begin and had to turn back.

chapter 8

GREAT CLUNK on his shoulder. Twenty years ago he'd have . . . The fire simpered, held in the log. May I go play outside? Catherine. She'd learned lots quickly. Had to. Suppose Lucia told her about all the great prisoners, Socrates, Gesù, Pierre e Paolo. Kung never jailed. Martyrdom no profession. Takes weight off own shoulders. What Occident could be if it faced up to itself. No chopped-up gods in China.

That lopsided flopper taking over the house. The invited host. Nearly knocked Catherine off her pins. Clapping my shoulder. Comes in with a caravanserai of kids. Attila of the pigsty.

Yet.

And the women. Lucia thinking he can keep me up to snuff. Oh yes, another Pardie.

Yet. In the dark, all us cats.

Pure hearts had brought disaster.

Not their fault. Kung. Andrea. Homero. Wolfgang. The

heart's tones. Ruffled wheatfield, white before storm, sky violet, blowing crowns, underside of beads. Memory. *Che un marmo solo in sè.* Hammer, chisel. The truth within the stone. Process. Pardie. Wild moon face. Time's sucker-up. Rode any wave. Kept on balls of his feet at seventy. Wacky, but a marvel. Like Mother and Dad. But they were wacky through me. See them arriving. Naples. Eyes little squares of hurt. Why hadn't I told them long before? "It's so beautiful, Thad."

"Better come ahead, Mother. You'll get conked by a trunk." Old fellow nearly did, dodged, glasses fell off. "Thanks, son. Don't look as if they can lift those things. Wiry bunch."

"Give 'em a bowl o' tripe once a week, they'll lift the ship out of the bay. Look over. In the clouds. Know what that is?"

"Vesuvius?"

"Bravo. You'll have no trouble."

His father younger then than he now, seven, no eight years. Mother must have been sixty-four. Or five. No. They landed on the eleventh, her birthday the fourteenth. In Girgenti they took over. The king and queen. When Pardie came, Dad told him he ought to read economics. "The world's burning up, Pardie. It's no time for landscapes." Pardie said it was the hair of the dog, five hours with me, then up with a swollen head and running smack into Dad. Died at the right time. Three years shy of the war. They had their fling. At the end of my rope.

The women. End of ropes. Bells, nooses. Nina. On the cookie-passer's rope. Ordinary women can swill hot air. But poets? Too old for rescue work.

"I'll never learn then." Catherine. Had it been like that? And the boys? Sent off. He and Joanna had spared themselves. Sculptor's dust in baby's lungs. Buonarotti had none.

The Pisani? Of course. Pardie said, "Raise him yourself." As if that were man's noblest work. "Men love what they see growing under their roof and show partiality." Poor Catherine. What counted was what you loved.

A letter from S. Walter Sloterman. What did the S. conceal? Have Guggenheim grant, write thesis on Tate and Oslo bronzes, coming to Venice, relatives there, like to drop in, chat at convenience, Jan. 18-22, anticipation extreme.

Why not? Failing grants, he was immobile, visible. Must be wonderfully alert to select a man's boyhood fumblings. Suppose only fanatics come to the island. And they find whatever they come to find. Sloterman. Assigned by Napoleon's officers to the nameless roughage. Ah well. Such jokes have bitten the jokers. Give them a generation, two, three. Henry said poetry would come crawling out of the ghetto. They say the new writers. Like the Irish, the Sicilians. But Gunther? Well and obscurely financed. Banker's son? Regarding one as source of stories, retold for *cunnus*. Some energy, much ease, a smidgen of brain. Table of contents without text. Corpsefingerer. Void curls to matter, uncurls, not mattering. Jot of friction-headed stuff turns gradually mind, love. And Gunther. Sloterman. Stitch.

He was uncurling.

Pardie painting till his eyes wore out, hand on Bull's face. Had never seen it. In England somewhere. Old Proust, for all the dungheap-kissing, kept to it till the wind was out. And he? Let Sloterman document it. What had he told the last interviewer? One of the apology-seekers. Why not? He had enough to apologize to the end of time for, and if he was not apologizing for what they thought he was apologizing for—

not having committed the sins they'd assigned him—let the apology suit their pinched shoe.

And let their tears rain forgiveness.

They ate up gloom. *Zeitgeist.* Open your insides for swine, then weep they're eating you. The Roosians. Rousseau-lickers. Ghetto writers. Now the wops. Kiss and tell, suffer and yell. One of them tried to make Sant' Ilario a diary. A giant Stitch from the gonads up. As if they'd never heard of Greece, Egypt. Know thyself. How that perverted them.

How could a sculptor displace what was in the stone? How could he feel the same way over months of hammering? Had they ever tried hammering fifteen hours a day for sixty years? Or minutes?

As if sculpture had but one side. Even Benvenuto saw forty-six sides in the figure. Though front and rear were all he remarked in the street. Where was he in the Salt Shaker? Where was Tino in the Charity? The babes sucking the wonderful ovoids. Like Brancusi's. Where was Brancusi in the Bird? Where was that Charity? The Bardini, maybe, but made for the Duomo. To be seen from twenty or twenty-five yards, eye to waist level. If he could see it.

Yes.

Pencil, paper.

Miserable drawing. Stroke, get mouth over nipple, nipple making form in mouth, mouth sphering nipple, yes, something like that, and into the north field with the Jefferson plow and the Indus figure. Agriculture, family, nurture, government, *pax.*

On the island, the wind driving the light across the waves, tickling, washing the stones.

No. Pointless. Legs shivering. *Troppo goffo pel Duomo.*

[85]

STITCH

Lucia. What's the matter? Yes, I'd better. Little tired. Wish you . . .

2

Sloterman was a squat, wobbly man of thirty-five with a great hunk of nose, and black, steel-ball eyes behind silver-rimmed thick spectacles. He wore a fur-collared, fur-lined overcoat, padded overshoes, fur earmuffs wired around his head under a gray fedora, and a muffler so involved with his teeth that if Miss Fry had not expected him, she would not have been able to understand the name he gave her. It took him a long minute to remove all this, and another to remove his suit jacket and sweater, fold the sweater over a package he'd brought and reassume his jacket. It was indeed cold in Venice, he said, but he'd just read a Venetian account of the winter of 1437, and he'd come "as I'm afraid you see," *prepared*.

He wobbled up the stairs after Miss Fry, and went over to the bed where Stitch lay under the brown blanket. "A great honor," he said in a low, toneless voice.

"Wha' was that?" Stitch staring greenly into the square, huge-nosed face stuck up gargoyle-like on the squat body. Sloterman repeated it more loudly, still tonelessly.

He sat at the foot of Stitch's bed, waiting without anxiety. After a few seconds, Miss Fry said, "Mr. Sloterman has come down from Paris."

"By way of Toulouse," said Sloterman. "Wanted to look at the capital you'd worked with on Sant' Ilario. Must have been two inches of snow fell while I stood there. Might as well have stayed in the train." He touched his glasses. "I tried without these, but then couldn't make out the snow. Went across to a shoemaker, asked if I could borrow a ladder. Ended up on a baby's high chair stuck on top a great pile of snow. Got my arms round the capital, put my face right to the little devil figure when the chair collapsed. Just fell away. Had a grip on the pillar, must have lasted a second or two up there. Sliding down, saw something circular, like a nickel, not carved, *stuck* between the toes of a littler devil curved in behind the other one. Thought of it sliding down, and digging myself out and through a night of sneezes on the train."

"A message from Ruskin saying 'I beat you,' " said Stitch.

"Ha," said Sloterman and took a piece of paper out of his pocket. "I've got four short questions. May I ask them?"

"Shoot." Stitch propped up his pillow and back.

"One. Did you cast the Third Grace yourself? Two. (a) Is it lost wax like the others, and if so (b) what went wrong? Three. Do you want it seen eye level or from a foot or more below? And Four. Did you use some of the sketches for the Oslo group?"

"One, no. Two, (a) No (b) there was a squirt in the foundry who thought he'd do me a favor. Three, I'd say about a foot, but I'm not fussy. And Four, The Oslo?" Sloterman nodded once, the glasses, weakened perhaps in Toulouse, bobbing loose on his great nose. "I think there's some connection, yes. There often is. Anything else?"

Sloterman shook his head. "No. That's good."

Miss Fry went down to make tea. Sloterman followed her. "Forgot something," and fetched the package from under his sweater. It was a cake, and more than that, a birthday cake with TS in pink sugar on a chocolate frosting. "Binding's brandy," said Sloterman to Miss Fry. "Thought that might be all right." He put the huge sphere on a tray.

"How marvelous," she said. "How marvelous of you. And it's a French cake. You've brought . . ."

"Paulthier's in Toulouse. It's an excuse for me. Love it. Had one ten years ago and never forgot it. Know I'm a week early, but couldn't resist sharing it with you."

It was indeed marvelous. Stitch and Sloterman each ate two great hunks, and there was general discussion about cakes that had been eaten over the past seventy-five years.

"Come again," said Stitch, shaking hands, "cake or not."

Sloterman had to meet his relatives and regretted not being able to stay for supper. He hoped he'd be back in June.

3

Cressida had had an idea which occurred within minutes of hearing from Edward's cousin Wallie that he would be in Venice for a few hours doing some work. According to Edward, Wallie was a plodder, but he had plodded his way into all sorts of fellowships and through at least three books, one of which he'd sent them. He was clearly learned, and though a veritable museum of ugliness, he apparently had some sort of place in the world. He was an art historian but made his living as consultant to a small foundation with headquarters in Santa Barbara.

It was Cressida's flash that of all the work in the world none would be more up Edward's alley than cultural work with a foundation. And why not Wallie's? Edward was a great reader, he liked to keep up on things in all the arts and had considerable knowledge of them although he himself wasn't capable of putting together two words, two notes, or two strokes of paint.

Her plan was simple. They would get Wallie to put in the strongest possible pitch at the foundation. Edward could do the rest. With a foundation job, he could even manage a few European jaunts which would get him out of her hair. Santa Barbara was supposed to be America's *Côte d'Azur*. No snow, no colds, nothing but an occasional earthquake to worry about. And keeping Quentin out of the waves. And sharks. It would be a place that would compensate for a lot of things.

Was the plan conditioned on her continuing to live with him? Not entirely. Why shouldn't he have a job that pleased him anyway? A lucrative one. Neither direct support nor alimony could be squeezed out of the stones of Venice.

The day before Wallie was due in, she talked to Edward. In these first weeks of the new year he'd been singularly mild, even domestic. He had gone shopping for her, not yelled at the kids, stoked the stove at night, and occasionally asked her opinion about something in the *Gazzettino*. She attributed the behavior to some form of annual resolution. Or could it be that her own resolution to put the house in order had been undertaken by powerful agencies? Anyway, if the change wasn't great enough to alter her feelings seriously, it did make living in the same house with him less of a strain.

He'd said, "I don't think there's much of a chance."

"A refusal still puts you one up on present plans."

By the time they sat in Harry's Bar, their rendezvous with Wallie, he'd come around to saying, "Why not? It's as good as another and better than Noonan." Though so quietly, she wondered if something had happened to him.

Edward had gone to Nina's the day after New Year's, his heart

[89]

full of wish to comfort her. Knives had flashed in the air. His
clumsiness, his inability to say what was needed. Nor had he
dared see Stitch after Christmas. He'd written a note to Miss
Fry saying it was clear he disturbed the man and, since he ad-
mired him so much, he would not come again unless sent for.
He had not been sent for.

Watching the canal waters lap the carved lintels of lower
stories, Edward felt the sympathetic misery of submergence.
Since New Year's, he'd almost hidden out on the Giudecca.
He stayed close to his obligations, it suited his feelings. As for
Cressida's fence-mending, let it fence in what was fenceable.

He was looking forward to seeing Wallie. He'd grown
up across Washington Park from him; which somehow counted
now. They were about the same age. Which also counted.
Though for years he'd regarded Wallie as a third-rate pedant:
his inability to stick with a university—he'd been an instructor
in the N.Y.U. Art Department and then had shifted to the
foundation—marked him as a weak sister. Edward attributed
the grants he got so regularly to foundation pull. As for his
articles and books, anyone seemed to get published, though the
one book of Wallie's he'd read was better than he'd have
guessed, an analysis of theories of perspective. The hand-me-
down of some scholar engaged in crucial matters; yet one
learned something from it. Wallie was a good mechanic.

He and Cressida sat around the curve of the bar, facing the
entrance, when Wallie pushed open the door. Or rather a five-
and-a-half foot pile of clothes surrounding a pair of frosted
spectacles pushed it open and goggled at the smoked interior.
Edward rose and shook its hand, brought it into the corridor,
and handed its inorganic components to the hat-check girl who

stored them away. Then over to the bar, where Cressida shook hands and brought the thawing face down to her cheek which was kissed without fuss. They moved to a table and Edward ordered for all of them in Italian, though even the Italians at Harry's sometimes ordered in English. "Best food in Venice, believe it or not."

"Our first meal here," said Cressida. "Or mine, at least."

Wallie said it was excellent, he'd been here a couple of times, and it was good to be back, how were the children, would they be up when he went across, for despite his protesting that he had a room at the Grand, they'd insisted on the phone that he come stay with them. He asked them about their Italian impressions, what it was like transplanting the children, and had they found any interesting people in town.

"A few," said Edward. "Not many, but a good few. In fact, maybe you'd be interested in meeting one of them, you'll never guess," and told him, then turned red when Wallie said he'd just been lucky enough to have a few minutes with him about business, but how he envied their opportunity to really know him.

Holy God, thought Edward. One never knows. The little bugger'll probably end up marrying the Grand Duchess of Luxembourg.

It seemed that there was nothing he could supply which Wallie lacked, though in blank openness Wallie continued to assert that everything he was told, everything he ate, everything he saw in their company was remarkable and precious and, thank God, he'd had to come down on business so he could be with sympathetic flesh and blood.

Edward relaxed into the edibles, inuring himself to their

cost by focusing on a figure so high that any bill would be a comedown. He didn't hear Cressida broaching her plan, or if he did, it was too roundabout for him to grasp. Wallie, however, saw it immediately, proclaimed it a wonderful idea, Edward would be perfect for the foundation, he would get to work back in Paris, and, in fact, would write a letter tonight preparing the way, he wasn't in Santa Barbara much himself, but it would speed his trips and ease his presence there if it worked out. They didn't know how hard it was for a man who loved families to be so unattractive he couldn't have one of his own. Which they both denied not only automatically but genuinely, for by this time the cousin shone with decency and appeal. "You're too good to choose quickly, Wallie," said Cressida.

To top their two hours there, Wallie took the bill. "It's expense money, and I haven't cost them a nickel so far. They'll fire me for avarice. And I don't have anything to do with my money anyway."

They were completely melted by him. Edward went to sleep thinking that this fatheaded little cousin was a prince of men, and when Wallie took off the next evening—he'd spent the day on Sant' Ilario—Edward rode to the station with him and saw him off. He also mailed the letter Wallie had written to the director of the Foundation. "Would a quarter of the world were a quarter as reliable," and his heart rose to the great muffled head bobbing out the window, the gloved hand waving as the train moved out.

❧ chapter 9

NINA DID NOT scare easily, but tonight, wrapped
in and around her red quilt, the heat low, the windows frosted,
she did not know whether or not she could make it. Her
Oklahoma money had gone, she hardly knew where, laundry,
stockings, a little booze, a few treats for the Gunther children.
(She'd not paid a lira of rent or of her *conto* at Bicci's.) She
was literally penniless, could not buy the underwear, bath
towel, or even toothbrush she'd needed for a week. You
couldn't charge or borrow a toothbrush, and with salesgirls
crawling over the stores, you couldn't steal one. She'd given
it a try in Standa, picking up a green one which blended into
the suit she wore, but on the verge of letting her sleeve swallow it up, she heard a salesgirl beyond eye range at her left
asking if there were anything else she wanted. She'd had to
inquire about "O'Shaughnessy brushes," the one she'd just
tested on her sleeve material not coming within twenty fibers
of the bristle content her teeth required. And she bared these

for the girl, an ugly, clearly maltreated type who would have snooped on the Pope. As for towels, she'd wrapped a couple of small ones around her waist after going to the toilet at Bicci's, but the genuine article, a fine, thick bath towel, was carried neither there, in the Gritti, nor in the three other deluxe rest rooms she tried. Venetians high and low understood poverty and guarded against its companion, theft. She got away with soap, so she didn't actually smell, though her teeth were yellow despite the salt she rubbed on them. Her room-and-a-half was hung with the stuff she washed every day, and the flapping of looped slips and torn panties was driving her crazy. Things didn't dry inside in Venetian winters, at least not in this one, the worst on record in Europe for sixty years. A cosmic conspiracy to drive her home. To break her.

It was breaking her. Her epic had stopped at Line One. The gods in the blue air had ice in their veins, the tree nymphs were stuck in the branch thorns, the Muses had bedded down with the hot-loined heroes for the winter. Nina was alone. She went like a robot to the Marciana but found she could read nothing but the botched English epics of the seventeenth century, miserable cut-rate imitations of Milton that far from putting her to sleep roused her to the only real feeling she had these days, disgust. In the morning she got up and faced herself in the little steamed-up mirror over the sink, bared her filthy teeth, pulled the skin down under her eyes, the veins thick and scarlet around the fuzzy blue spheres, her nose fat-winged around pug's gross nostrils, hair wildly scattered over the assertive forehead. "Hello, my beauty," she said to it. "Charted the day's great course?" Only vestigial will prevented return to the battered quilt.

For emphasis, she was alone. Edward hadn't shown up since

the day after New Year's when she'd thrown him out on his insensitive ear. Oskar was off in Milan and Genoa drumming up trade for his *pensione*. She had seen Fabio and Jaska but couldn't talk to them more than five minutes. And to cap it all, Charley was clearly gone for good. People still came to her with news of black-and-white dogs seen in all parts of the city, but, after half-hour hikes, they turned out to be gray or on someone else's proper leash. The only results were fatigue and further wear and tear on her underthings.

Then today, after weeks of not seeing hide nor hair of him, she talked with Stitch, and he'd come up with this strange proposal which had passed through her vacancy without resistance, but which now, as she lay under the miserable quilt, legs against her chest to fight the leaking chill, seemed a further assault on her debility.

In the Piazza, as she was coming out of the Marciana after a mind-stunning swallow of *Azaria and Husha,* Nina spotted him walking in the strip of sun flanking Quadri's; she was mooning along in the chill shade near Florian's. In his black cape and great-brimmed black fedora, he looked like a pensioned Dracula.

He spotted her and waved. Which she returned, and was going on when she remarked his black boots swerving around in paramilitary left face, heading toward her. She changed direction and beat him to the middle of the Piazza, where they stood, he in the sun, she not, and refusing the extra step that would bring her there till he faced around and forced her to face him. "I've missed you," he said.

"And I you. Have you been well?"

The beard tossed, the eyes threw up green crystals from the depths behind the straggly eyebrows. "In my time." That seemed

[95]

to be it, and as she had little to say and no ambition to say it, she began with a "Well," when he added, "Come with me to dinner tonight. Lucia's turned the tables and wants to rest. We can go to the Amici della Musica afterwards."

Invitations were never too frequent to dampen Nina, and this one, in the midst of her terrible gloom, was like forty degrees up the thermometer. She smiled without showing her teeth. The old man too seemed delighted. Clear pleasure, gain on all sides. Goodness, what was gloom when ten words could make life hop? They shook hands, and Nina watched him walk off with the church as backdrop, domes, horses, mosaics, gold and green and bronze and the cupolas graying pink. The rest of the Square was a bit melancholy, the pigeons moseying along between official feeds, only a few tables out in front of the cafés, but still, a home away from home, a great old dear like the cane-swinging Stitch. What a place. Yes. She went home, mind stirred up with the difference between "space" and "place," *"piazza"* and *"spazio," "place"* and *"espace."* She didn't eat lunch, banking on the dinner she would have with Stitch. As the afternoon went on, she began a sestina on the words *space, place, Venice, red, kind,* and *water.* It went slowly, but it went. In two hours, two lines out of seventy survived. Yet at three, the time she'd take Charley for a walk, she was miserable again; that scrapping, troublesome, ambulant affection. She stopped working. At the 3:30 bells, she thought Cammie and Brose, out of school now, might come over, and she boiled water for tea. Once or twice a week they came up to talk, but since New Year's they hadn't shown up. Maybe something had happened. But she would not call: spinster's constraint. She picked up Simone Weil's *La Pesanteur et la Grâce* and got as far as *"Deux forces regnent sur l'univers: lumière et pesanteur"* when a cry came through the French doors, Cinamundi, the fruit man, calling the right turn at the Fenice. She opened up to the chill and yelled, *"Ha visto il mio canino?"*

"'ente, sig'nina Nina. Dispiash'. 'ente." A bent clip of a man working the big oar of the *sandolino*, his crates covered better than he against the chill, shaking his black head sadly for her loss, rounding the corner.

It was the only talk she had that afternoon.

At five it didn't matter. She was lost in *pesanteur* and *lumière*, the former "place" the latter "space." Her sestina took off with them, she had two stanzas, and was juggling a line about "the mind's weight in this place," when the bell brought her back to time and hunger. *"Chi è?"* she called, sounding the entrance buzzer, and the old man waved with his cane and started up. "With you in a minute," and she scooped her wash off the lines, piled her note paper into a drawer, took up her driest hand towel, and leaped into the bathroom.

She apologized for being without a drink to serve him. "I've just run out," though she hadn't had anything in the house for a week.

He held up her red cape, and when she got into it, held her arm at the elbow until they got into the traghetto and crossed the canal for Bicci's.

Stitch was as hungry as Nina, which kept them wordless during the main dishes, but over coffee he leaned toward her, his beard grazing the yellow cheese which stood high beside his cup, and said quietly, "What do you have to do with this lopsided rhino?"

"Huh?"

[97]

He did not repeat it, but leaned back, once again grazing the cheese, palming the thin reddened bowl of a wineglass, smiling foxily at her over the great knot of his cravat in the Byron collar. She felt an answer extracted against her wish.

"Do? He's a friend. I don't have a great many. He's a decent fellow." Though she hadn't been thinking this lately. The answer was protection against that soft malice with which Stitch had amused himself on Christmas. If she'd been doubtful, the present characterization settled it.

Stitch's lips pursed within the hair. He rocked forward a little, and she looked up from the last spread of cheese. He said, "Wonder if they have any of that open apple cake?" Edward had served his sentence.

The waitress brought them double slices. "Sicilian apples," he said, gorging. "Formic. Ants in the bark." And told her a story of making a pilaf for a party in Girgenti, cheered by all, until they saw ants crawling out of each other's mouths. "Never tried doing it on my own, and could never have thought of it by myself. How about the Amici?"

"I don't think so," but she'd walk him to the concert.

He said he wouldn't go either, but could use a walk and would go back with her. They passed into the dark calle to get the traghetto.

It was there, under a small, bulb-lit Madonna fixed on the wall, that he stopped her, put his hand under her chin, the stiff fingers reaching up the jawbone to her left ear. His eyes glistened, collecting light at the shadow edge. She forced herself to hold still, to stare back at his eyes, thinking, He's shown his hand now. For fifteen or twenty seconds, maybe longer, she held her breath. "I think I could try the head," he said quietly, still holding it into the bulb's light. "The bone's close to the socket, there's a strong horizontal, the ear's subtle, it'll hold light." And then the—what? Request? Command? Statement? "I'd like to make the head."

Nina, looking through the line of shadow into the green fires, heard herself saying, "This head? Sculpted?" and going on, though there was no commitment, clarification, even motion outside the blinking green fires, "What an honor."

Home, under the quilt, the offer turned around so often in her head she was not completely certain it had been made, Nina wondered what—beyond velleity—was its point? Was it bad sign or good? That is, was she ready to be fixed in bronze or stone? Now, when her mind could barely work itself into a canzone, when she had to use it for shaking money out of some tree or other even to survive, when she didn't even know from day to day whether she could make it without doing what would almost take more courage than not surviving: throwing herself on Francis L.'s silent, transatlantic irony to beg for funds? If she had fifty dollars for towels and underwear and a little booze, she could hold out till the tourists showed up in the Piazza. Then she'd clean up with a sketch pad. Jaska hadn't cornered the market. But fifty was a million. Dog days. Dogless dog days. Rhino-less days.

What did the old man have against Edward? Could he possibly—it didn't seem—it didn't have any of the marks she recognized, but the annals displayed incredible varieties, who knew, maybe, just maybe he was trying to corral her.

Absurd. One whiff and she was off thinking the world's males from nine to ninety were asniff at her.

Within arm's reach, dripping slip, wool stockings, ripped panties. Trousseau. *Même pour un Rousseau insuffisante.*

On the traghetto, the gondolier's breath had smoked between her and Stitch, he standing at the pier waving to her, then giving the cape a guardsman's whirl and heading down the calle.

Where was she going to suck her next month from? Him? No. Neither him. Bicci? Oskar? Fogleman? Fogleman had sutured the wound; someone had told her about Charley, and the nearest thing to warmth available there had come dehiscent from the pod. She'd even wanted to put an ad in the *Gazzettino*. But would she shell out three hundred lire for a pair of underpants? Ixnay. Why? Really, why? She wanted humans as defenseless as animals. Civita would be easier. No. What if she got sick? Wait, that might do. But she'd seen the hospitals; she'd sooner die under her dripping underpants.

2

No, he didn't have the energy, the interest to make even the nose. Ten years ago, five, three, the girl might have stirred him enough to place her in the scheme with the other muses and spurs. A caryatid for the hint of Erechtheon in the east center, a ladder of zygomatic arches calculated for the April dawnlight, a support which was ascent, subordinating what it supported. To get her head there, the brave rise from the neck trunk, the flesh weave over feeling avenues, the smaragdine chips in the field-blue irises, the demi-dumbheaded push toward what he had so many years pushed toward. He did have his finger-itch, the stonecutter's malady, with which old Rotten-Good had swollen the hand of his giant-killer.

But the main thing was not himself for a change . . . for a change . . . but the little *Irische Kind* who was getting tangled in the lines of the poor slob and his domestic sty. Between the stiff one up the front and the soft ones at her side, she was going to think it worth something, and with any old fool in any place or other. He could, yes, serve. Not the body politic this time, nor any body, including his own. But her. If she showed up every day, while he made at least the motions of slapping clay on an armature, he would talk to her. She was worth more than the interviewers. Even the Slotermans.

The moon over the canal had suffered injury. Blotched and pale. *Contrista, conturbata.* Cynthia. Spheres are prone and erect at once. No moon on Sant' Ilario. Pocked dust, rock, light-stealer. Virgin huntress, chased and blotched. Do it with the girl's cheek.

Do it? It was a logistics miracle getting the fork in his teeth.

Good night, Nina, unvoiced, though his mouth smoked. From the canal she waved back. Nina. *Jimena, commo a la mie alma.* In sun, yet always shadowed, under the plane tree. Alberta, in the Diocletian, eyes from the marble limbs to each other's. Lucia, singing, *"J'ai une cuer trop lait, Qui souvent mesfait."* Joanna's well-bred passion. Pardie said, "Summer never touches her." Where? In Chancery Lane. Economics-Tuesday, Art-Friday, Signor Rotamundi flavoring the pasta with his whiskers. L.O.: "And this is what we're trying to save?" Fritz: "You see wot the Welsh snovabitch tole the ryle-roads?" L.O.: "Can a director of the Bank of England *tombe amoureux?"* Fritz, negative. Stitch, negative.

"Sera professore." Adela, stepping to the wall, bowing deeply; respect and its lampoon. Stitch walked past Bicci's and Calle Ramigero into the Zattere, where, face to face with the red-scarred moon, he felt his head clear up. For a few minutes the beauty of the water, the lit sky, the boats, the curve of the Giudecca, eased him.

❦ chapter 10

I N THE first week of February Edward went out to
Stitch's island. He'd held off till now, partly in sustained in-
fantile reaction to Nina's breaking her word to go there with
him, partly because he didn't want to be stuck for the three
hours' wait between boats with no café to sit in, no fresh newspapers, magazines, *pasticcerie*.

He was the only one who got off at Sant' Ilario. The ACNIL
man said he hoped he wouldn't be cold, it was going to snow.
"See you at two-thirty."

"Good-by," said Edward, a little afraid now on this scraped
bone stuck into the throat of the granular, air-quivering lagoon.
He climbed the hill and the gray began condensing into a
silver mist of snow.

Edward looked through it, down. "Holy Jesus."

Stranded, antique, a paleolithic city, red, silver, pink, blue,
gold.

"So-o-o, this is it. This is what it's about." He descended, down by the fish-wall, by a minaret-pyramid, by shelves of figures, plowshapes, an aluminum river, heads he knew, half-heads he half-knew, nonheads that were heads, bodies and bodylike nonbodies, scenes, stone events, a fair of blazing rocks, a Last Supper of eyes. An endless maze of solids conjured out of colored earth-stuff. In and out he walked, now touching, gilding, sparking the stones.

Stitch's world.

It annexed Edward, sometimes with passion, occasionally with disgust (gross buggery, scatalogical caricature); always, it moved, slow shuttle between intimacy and distance.

For two hours Edward walked and looked without more than three thoughts of anything other than what he saw. Then, while looking emptily at a kind of limestone gallbladder, something hammered the back of his neck: fatigue. A mind-cracking fatigue. His legs were lard, his feet dead cold in his rubbers, his mouth sand. He reached for the rose-flecked marble arms of a crucifix-woman and held there for minutes, head against its sleeted semi-head.

Strength rose in him, his head cleared. He got up the hill, and decided not to turn around. "I've had it. God knows I've had it."

It had stopped snowing. Far out he saw the boat stitching the lacerated skin of the lagoon.

2

The morning after New Year's, Edward had gone in to Nina's. When she opened the door, he'd said "Well?"

A natural, a classical ellipsis, but it triggered a most unnatural response. She'd removed his arm from her own like a thread and said he must not become excited, birth was indispensable to all he cared for, it originated in the noblest impulses he would ever know, he must not let money worries interfere with his indulgence of it; plus which, he hadn't properly come in, wasn't he even going to take off his overcoat, he was so expert a remover of clothes.

All in a quiet, reportorial manner that he wouldn't have guessed could be as alien to her as it was. Hearing it, he realized that her voice was usually full of breath, pitch slides and climbs, a speech, of whose richness he'd been unaware until the flatness of her uncordial, unreassuring reassurance. Which he met not in kind but with conscious subdual of his resentment at it. "I'm not excited, Nina. Nor do I think we need make a comic opera of it."

" 'O reason not the need,' " said Nina.

He bypassed this bypass. "As you say, it is an important business, and I'm entitled to know where we stand."

"What analytic and expressive gifts are yours, Mr. G." Flat, but far more direct, which gave him some leverage. Though, after all, the poor little trot was probably scared to death. He took off his coat, of which she didn't relieve him and which he resisted throwing on the chair and just held. "Easy, Neen. I take it you haven't had it yet."

Nina's teeth, yellow and sharp, were exposed, fiercely. Each word of her answer was cut out and delivered from a chill block of fury. "What-in-hell-is-it-to-you? Keep-your-questions-and-penis-out-of-me." A horrible odor from the filthy teeth. Skin-shrinking. "Why don't you go on back to your official hole?"

"Listen, Nina," but to what? He left.

And hadn't seen her since. Each day he thought a call might arrive with the message she knew he expected, plus any apology she happened to have handy; but when it didn't, he thought he'd starve her—of both company and funds—into submission. As for the crucial matter, no news was usually good news. Now, on the boat coming back from Sant' Ilario, he felt he had to see her. Nina, he wanted to say, Nina, I've seen it. I've felt it. It's something marvelous. They would come together over it, sharing insights. Artistic and intellectual communion, with affection for mortar. This was what great works did. They made a community, men against the chill.

He got off and ran to Santa Maria del Giglio. No one there. She was probably in the Marciana. He started for it, but then went back to the newsstand woman in the campo and asked her if she'd seen the little American signorina. Yes, she'd gone toward San Stefano half an hour ago. Maybe she was taking her laundry. "Did she have any packages with her?"

"Non signore, niente."

Perhaps she'd gone over to Bicci's for lunch. He took the traghetto over, walked up to Bicci's and looked in. She was not there. On impulse he went on up the fondamenta to Calle Ramigero, to Stitch's door. He had his fist raised to knock, when he thought, Even if she's here, I've got no right to call. And at lunchtime. But he would have liked to see Stitch, to tell him what he'd just seen and felt out on the island. A light came from the downstairs room through the crack of the hooked storm shutters. Edward pulled himself up on the window ledge and looked in. There was Nina in a red skirt and sweater; in front of her, at the right, was a table on which stood some twisted wire, and to the right of this was Stitch, leaning forward, smiling at Nina, his hands on the wire. Edward stared, amazed, then lost his grip and fell to the ground. Slush slopped his Loden and pants. Fear of being discovered sneaking by Stitch or Nina propelled him to his feet, and he dashed out of the alley and walked rapidly, head down, along the fondamenta. A yard from Bicci's a figure skirted his advance. "Ah, Mr. Gunther." Miss Fry, with a great bag of groceries.

"Yes, good morning," said Edward, and averting his head, went into Bicci's breathing hard, asweat, unconscious of his abruptness until he'd sat down at a table and then, so upset by it, he left before eating and headed back for his bed on the Giudecca.

Passing Calle Ramigero again, something touched his shoulder.

"Hello, Edward."

Nina. Blushing for that spying self flat on its aching back, his first impulse was continued flight toward home, his second, to kiss her. His third repressed his second. Nina. A warming fire in this miserable winter. Red cape, pink cheeks, her smile driving dimples into them, eyes almost violet with depth, the brightest thing in Venice. "I've missed you," she said.

"And I you, Nina. Very much. I didn't dare call after last time."

"I thought you'd given me up. I was so hard on you. Forgive me. I don't know how to treat lovers."

"I almost forgot."

"You know I was worried last time. Which fouls up the period. And I'd just lost Charley. I'm almost used to it now.

Anyhow, I've missed you, Eddy. You're looking good, you've lost weight."

"Exercise. And eating at home. Cressida can't even pour Corn Flakes right. How's—" and he jerked thumb and head back toward the calle.

"O.K."

"I heard somewhere he was making a head of you."

"Yes," easily, but looking up so suddenly her head nearly conked him in the jaw. "I go to pose now and then. He needed a woman for something or other on the island. I was glad to see him working again." Her arm, out of the slit in her cape, went around his, and they walked toward the traghetto and took it across the canal. He aimed at her calle but she turned him right toward the café in front of the Ponte Ostreghe. The canal in low tide bore a rash of garbage, orange peels, slats of packing crate, a piece of red cloth, a cover of *Epoca* (the Pope and Khrushchev's son-in-law grinning wetly at each other). They stood arm in arm on the top step surveying the garbage. Peace, thought Edward. It doesn't take much.

Inside the little café—asteam from the silver espresso cylinders —they ordered two *macchiati*. Nina, cape doffed, put her forearm over Edward's. "I haven't spoken to anyone I care about since New Year's." He flushed with pride. "It usually doesn't bother me. It hasn't mattered whether I was with someone or not. But now things are running against the grain. My money's run out. I can't get any jobs around here. Nothing. I even stole a toothbrush from Stitch's. Things are low."

"You've never looked better, Nina." Her face was rosy, fruit-ripe and, yes, her teeth were white.

"The sky before the storm. I'm close to asking my father to

lend me enough to get home. Starting over. Maybe I'd make it the second round."

"Why don't you get one of these fellowships?"

"Big yuk. I've been turned down three times. Stitch says they turned him down too. And every person he ever recommended. They're not geared to us."

Edward shifted with this identification, but his arm and head, surmounted by hers, were fixed; her soft fingers on his short, deep-webbed hand, an intimacy. But he said, "Paranoia. Good people have gotten them."

"Impossible. Who would tell they were any good? O.K. It's sour grapes. Anyway, I don't want a patron. I've paid my own freight for twelve years. Screw 'em all."

"At least there's natural endowment. Here's all I got." And he drew his arm from under hers and pulled out tax forms he'd picked up at the consulate. "I've had no income in nine months. Except a hundred bucks' worth of savings interest. Now I've got to bleed the air and come up with taxes." He held up two fingers. "And each month two households draw on me. Five people. Not counting Lydia. Why does the government need me? I've paid for my sins. God paid me to start with, with the old minus sign."

"And I thought you could lend me money. We're a poor lot. We better get Adela to take us in. Do you have enough for a sandwich?"

He held up two fingers at the sandwich counter. *"Uove-carci-ofó, per piacere, Signora.* And I can give you twenty bucks, Nina. Might as well go down together."

"I don't want it, Eddy. But you can swipe me a good towel and give me about a thousand lire. Maybe two. I'm ashamed to

tell you what for. No, I'm not. Kotex. No thanks to you."
With a sweet laugh. "A few more days and I'd have had to
stay in bed. It's the lowest."

"Must be why there are so few women tramps." He took
out his wallet, fingered a five, but then gave her a 10,000 lire
note. "I wish there were a lot more, baby."

"I'm grateful beyond words, Eddy. You'll mark the difference. Money means more than people who just work for it
know. It's like a secret script. *Rongorongo.* A few people understand it, and they run things. I'm with Stitch there. If I
gave a damn about it, I'd do something. I do give a damn, but
it's not the whole story. Nature's under money, and it'll bury
it." She held her fist up, the 10,000 poking out in fragments.
"I'm grateful for this, angel. I'm enough in the money world
to respect being clean. Let alone stopping my lady wounds."

Edward regarded her little pug face absorbed in its moneyed
fist. "Nina," he said, his voice hoarse, "would you marry me?"

She looked quickly into his face, her eyes blue flares. Laughing. "Would you support me?"

"Now and then."

She got up, clipped on her cape at the neck. "Well, it'll give
us something solid to talk about."

3

Marriage.

He was married. He had three children by his wife. They'd
spent five thousand days together, a hundred thousand hours.
One loved what one should love. Oh yes. Stories would go
out of life if it were so.

STITCH

It came to Edward, walking beside Nina, almost walking over her, his great Loden casting a brown shadow on her rose-round cheeks, that he did, spasmodically, love her, yes, though as escape, open door to hopes he hadn't earned. And something else came: the pressure to tell her that what he'd seen on the island embodied his own fault, not mindlessness, but the lethal haste of passion, hunger, ambition. Admirable as Stitch's breadth was, a marvel and wonder of work and sympathy, maybe it was what the old man had said himself, "Scattered notes." Scattered by uncontrolled desire. Beautiful, artful, but flotsam.

The greatest men exhausted what they touched, but Stitch fingered, hinted, compared, abandoned. His island was beautiful wreckage. Really great men were mad for what they treated, could not get enough of it, pored over it, smothered the world with its qualities. Their only control was their need to offer it. One felt the power of their love; so personal, it penetrated even the alien. Yes. The greatest were not anonymous, communal. Their love churned their own stuff into constellations, creatures. And what counted after the greatest spurt of nature, conception—that packaged history of matter —was the interweaving of the creature with speech, gesture, song, knowledge, with what had been. You could look at life large or small. Artists had to look at it large, too large to be lovingly recorded except in detail. Which is where Stitch failed. Stitch's great gifts, his technical skill, sense of form and mimic power made his work stunning, a marvel, but he was not among the greatest, and anyone who followed him, lacking his marvelous energy, eye, strength, curiosity, and tenacity, would create monsters. Stitch's life, as well as his island, marked the generality of his passion. He was always leaving things out, abandoning them, as he had his children. Maybe that was why, in his daughter's presence, he had lashed out Christmas Day.

Walking into Campo Santa Maria del Giglio, Edward swelled with his insight. He had come on something crucial for Nina. Something that would rescue her from the Stitchian world. Helpless himself, unable to hold a hammer or hear a rhythm, his life could take form guiding his superiors. This was the core of his marriage proposal. It was means, not end. Softened by passion, Nina would take the imprint of his insight.

4

"But no," said Nina. "No one respects what's been more than yours t., but, Edward, *mon cher fils,* that reeks of graves. You've been drinking morgue dust. We've exhausted the Flamands, Zola, the wart-and-molars, Rodin, Herr Strauss. There's too much stuff in the universe. One must hint, skim, move around, suggest. A highlight here, a detail there. One must pay tribute to the over-all, not wallow in the singular. I'm with Stitch. Suggest, renew, compare, diversify, and cheer what's in front of your face. Depth analysis is for birdbrains. One must select, refine, bore tunnels into the great light. Like this garbage canal." They were on the Ponte del Dose, another scheme of garbage floating for inspection. "You overlook it and what do you see?" Ahead, the sun touched silver veins in the Grand Canal. "The main stream beyond the garbaged vertical, that's what. The cross on the 'T' which makes more than another 'I.' "

STITCH

"Apply my analogy," said Edward, face as fired in its darkness as Nina's in its rose-speckled fairness, his gloved hand clutching air for emphasis, his eyes gripping hers in debater's passion. Didn't she want to be saved? "You gonna throw children into this abstract hash machine too?"

"They're there now. Personality's washed out of the world. There's no room for it. Find me a Dickens world today. You can't. The Dickens people are in the loony bins where the starch is taken out of them quick. There's not enough elbow room for the singular. I'm not saying it's good, but let's face it, that's the way of things. The human condition will obtain, but in other ways, other modes, according to the Great Scheme."

"But, Nina!" shouted Edward. A little man as humped as the bridge they stood on shot a trembling rodent's head at him as he scrambled down away from the rush of non-Italian pouring from the mountainous foreigner. "You're bundling singularity away. You're stuffing particulars into ovens, baking them all under one crust."

"No. Wrong. The crust isn't common. Every cook makes it different. Despite similarity of ingredients, the things which count don't change. If the consumer's subtle enough, he can distinguish a cook in one bite. But that doesn't matter. The idea's to get the mass of what counts and a mite of clearly seen detail. You can't let yourself get lost in detail. Stitch is on to that. But he's a pioneer, and full of tics, so his work's imperfect. I don't mean mine'll be perfect, but I mean he's still got a foot in the School of Singularity. Look at his own heads and his girl friends' cropping up out there on the island. They're unassimilated to the over-all as far as I can see. But his general procedure is marvelous, and he can set one off. Eddy, it isn't just the artificial world, the world of *tekné*. It's the whole world. Look at your own troubles. Look at mine. Where do they come from? Leaks in the general. Maldistribution of goods. Attempts to be what we aren't. Overprizing our singularity. Egoism. Imperceptivity in situations solved long ago. Failure to adapt. The bloodline runs from the world to art's expression of it. Like this filth-ridden canal into the great one out there."

Little blue-eyed babe. Who was she to contain all this? "Come on," he said. "I can't think with you screaming at me," and walked her down through Campo San Stefano, past peach-colored palaces and the brick church the color of his Loden, down under the weak sunlight following the long snake curve of the canal, behind the ins and outs of palaces, their backsides swallowed by canal water, their walls disguised by bare shrubs, trees, chewed-up stone faces. "You're making a fatal error," he told her. "You must be wrong. You're violating life. You're a Utopian, a Platonist. Artists must be more human, not less. And human is failing. They all fail. Look at old Stitch, stuck in that tiny place, freezing his miserable bones; one of every seven or eight days in his life spent in the pokey. That's not failure of the general. That's a thrust of the particular too big to be held by the—by the general arteries. Artists don't mirror the times. They create new time out of the powerful digestion of what's around them." Pause. "Look at me."

As example? No. He stopped her, held her by the elbows. They were in a little pipe of alley, against a plum-colored palace wall, the air above thinly, gaseously gray, turning black as it slipped between the walls.

Nina faced him, the vessels behind her cheeks and temples

emptying, her eyes huge now, staring up at him, not laughing, her lips, almost detached, pink like some odd internal organ, untouched. Like a mountain over her, he bore down, brought his thick deer-brown arms around her. The red cape crushed into cloth waves, his dark head under the blocked green felt coming down like a storm on her, while she met his lips, the green brim crumpling, falling off, and their faces rubbing against each other, sucking each other, feeling the sealy muscle of each other's tongue, groaning, fighting for breath. Oh, what discourse. What a symposium. Nina, bent against the stone, bruised under the cloth, feeling his heaviness, but overall, feeling that same terrible surge she had felt on New Year's Eve.

There were no taxis, no rapid transits in Venice, emergency treatments were at the mercy of water. They walked as fast as possible, only a little of their passion leaking away. The dialogue was over. Back through the streets, a stop-off for Edward at Farmacia Stefano Martir, past Santa Maria del Giglio, and, double pace now, into Nina's calle.

chapter 11

Though he'd had a blowup last night, shouting like a maniac at Brose, knocking his fist against the wall till the fury died in his face, it *was* the first time in weeks; and it had been the *wall*, not Brose. Then too the children *did* bait him, particularly Brose. Last night he'd kept calling him "Hippodad" despite storm warnings.

The main thing was that he was thinking seriously about next year. He talked about California as if it were a natural extension of Wallie's generosity. Meanwhile, he was apparently working at something. At least he spent a few hours every day in front of his green portable slamming its diminutive keys against the yellow paper he'd swiped pads of from Noonan's. Dressed in his blue polo coat, he brooded before the machine, a bear swiping at mushrooms. If she or Quentin came in, there would be a scene of quiet sufferance: his head would shift away from the ruinous noise, ear cocked in a tension of delicacy.

Yes, it wasn't impossible that they were going to make it

together. He was clearly trying. He volunteered to shop, and occasionally she let him, despite his—it amounted to—talent for getting the wrong thing in the wrong quantity, rice for potatoes, rolls for bread, altogether forgetting the meat. Or was he too lazy to wait in the stores?

Anyway he appeared to try. Also, he was eating less and doing push-ups twice a day, stomach reaching the carpet inches ahead of his chest. He felt harder to her, and this comforted more than physically: it was as if the Edward she'd first known had been deformed by haphazard accretions and was now trying to regain his real shape. Cressida knew you didn't recover what you lost, people weren't newts. But she did not ask for more than recognizable continuity, which now seemed a possibility.

She began taking more time for herself, shopping in town, sightseeing. A little at a time, but with savor. She left Quentin to Lydia and took herself off to palaces, museums, churches. These were invariably moist and drafty, but she never stayed long, and discomfort only increased the pleasure of the lunches she took at her leisure in the first decent trattoria spotted after sightseeing. Alone, or occasionally with Edward, and two or three times with Brose and Cammie at a place near their school, Cressida enjoyed the pleasure of someone else's cooking, the attention of male lunchers, and the ease with which a cool look deflected their warmer ones.

For so long she'd considered herself as rooted as a flower. Indeed she'd wondered how a flower felt under the bee's hairy belly. Who knew if evolution would not turn up a bee-refusing flower? Its beauty would be a distant treat, untouchable. Why was she an availability, a commodity? Why was her most powerful strategy not rational but physical refusal? Had she made an initial mistake with Edward? Or was he the sort of man with whom rational give-and-take was impossible? Years ago he'd given her the Freudian prescription of male dominance. It had persuaded her completely. But what did a nineteenth-century Viennese Jew have to do with the way she lived? Had she ever threatened Brose with castration? Absolutely not. Yet Edward, under Freud's aegis, ruled the roost. His moods, his desires, his dislikes. She hadn't eaten a beet in eleven years, and she loved them. She hadn't even ordered them in restaurants. Their odor sickened him. All right, she could be beetless. It didn't matter, and hundreds of other minor deprivations didn't matter. Even his dominance didn't matter. But what did matter was the give-and-take which meant that the partner, yes, partner, was agreeable, loving, even neat (i.e., practiced the simple virtues that made a woman think the household really counted, that she counted).

How had Adrienne felt? Cressida had always taken Edward's view of the divorce; monthly alimony payments made it easy. Yet Edward had married her as well as divorced her. There must have been a minimal decency. Why had he divorced a more or less decent woman?

The world's Edwards, men of minimal accomplishments and fair intelligence, were always mercurial. Even in the best years of their marriage she had sensed the tension of Edward's resignation, the resentment of his own ease. Then, in Europe, the resentment mastered him. And she'd become, as Adrienne had become for him, an object. Years ago, when she'd asked him to describe Adrienne, he'd said she was dark, a trifle oily, thin, fairly pretty *à la juive*. As if the woman were a painting. How had she been described to the chick he'd carted off to

Cuma? "Oh yes, fattish, high-breasted, clear-faced, pretty *alla* Anglo-Irish."

She sat in a trattoria near the Accademia by a window over-looking a palace which sported an oval medallion, winged lion with smashed wings, eyes and nose crushed stonily into each other. A film of noonlight softened it. Nearby, canal noises, boats, cries. Eating, Cressida lost herself in the sounds and sights, a depth of peace which warmed and intoxicated her. After lunch she went into the museum and looked at the St. Ursula pictures.

In this hour with the Carpaccios, there had been no boundary between her mind and the birds, boats, arches, figures, towers, plants. It was as if her intimacy with them had been a previsioned substitute, or more, as if the hour were instructing her in her own resources, even soliciting the independence it showed she had at her command. "As if I'd already thought I could make it alone."

Half an hour later, walking over the Accademia bridge, she saw Edward and Nina rushing hand in hand across Campo San Stefano, then Edward alone pushing in and out of the Farmacia Stefano Martire, and while she watched from the top step of the bridge, hardly more disturbed than surprised, she saw them look oddly into and then away from each other's faces and move, no, run, arm in arm through the calle which led to Santa Maria del Giglio.

2

Edward came home early for supper. Brose and Cammie were playing a version of hopscotch with three other children. The sun was breaking up against the western rim of the lagoon, and the curve of fondamenta where the children played was masked in a golden afterlight. In jackets, hats, scarves, the children, far off, looked as if they were on stage. Edward stood at the pier watching them hop, turn, stoop, call out. Beyond them was San Giorgio Maggiore's tower, carved out of the pink loam of southern sky, so beautiful it felt like another child to him. He took off his right glove, flexed his fingers against the chill, and put them to his forehead, pushing up his green hat brim. He was both so much at peace and so confused. Venice, heart-rendingly beautiful, his children like natural aspects of it, and his own bulk, floating in ease, yet resentful of that body which supplied it.

Which was the source of his confusion. A protection, perhaps, against thinking through the irreconcilability of his attachments. Walking from Nina's, waiting for the vaporetto, the fuzz had been streaked by a thought of Stitch's domestic life, a harmony of the same elements which discomposed his. Why wasn't he that self-sufficient? The only thing he wanted to surrender was his trouble. Up and down his cheek, against the tiny bristles of his beard, then into his ear and around the labyrinth, Edward's forefinger moved instead of his mind. And then, with a breath so deep, the cold seemed to take a nip of his lung, he walked slowly home working the stiffness out of his face, readying it for smiles. "*Ciao,* Pop." Brose on one leg, from the interior of a chalked rectangle. Cammie ran to him, cheek tilted toward his lips.

He had to force himself to oblige. Nina's body, powerful, odorless, was still on his lips. It was not something to transmit to his little dark beauty. But he did, then went off into the courtyard, took courage from the harsh drip of the fountain, the nude, thorny sadness of the soil. He climbed the steps by the frieze of cats, conscious of each step, fourteen of them, he'd not counted before. In front of the door, looking at the brass knocker, a dog's head, yellow tongue for thumping, he'd not noticed that either. He opened up and took in Warm Morning's cindery heat.

"Hi, Cress." His voice broke over this, it came out "Hi-ness." No answer. Shopping. Whew. He hung his coat on the gilded rack, opened the study door, felt its chill with relief, got the first book in reach, *The Mystery of Edwin Drood,* and went up the other hall toward his room.

She was lying on her bed, face toward the wall, dressed, her backside aimed at him. He regarded it dispassionately, then went to his own bed, manipulated the lamp cone above it, and had just read the first sentence of the Introduction, "Edwin Drood is a mystery within a mystery," when he heard, "Get out." Not loud, but as if the two words had lots of syllables.

He shut the book over his forefinger, stared at the cover, a grainy blue ersatz leather, then put its coolness against his eyes. He said nothing, only took a breath and held it for five or six seconds.

"Get out. 'Get out,' I said."

His head separated from her feet by two slabs of oak, his headstead, her footstead. He did not look around, but asked as quietly as he could manage, "What's the matter?"

"Out. Out. G-e-t o-u-t. You know. You know what you've been doing. You and that smelly poet. I'm so fed up I can't. Get out!" This a scream, as if her head had just come off. The courtyard must have heard that one. The whole Giudecca.

He jumped up, went around to her bed, stood over her till she sat up, face chalky, eyes blue bulges, sweat drops showing under the fair line of hair roots. He held up his hand, the blue book in it, waved it. "Shhhh, shhhh. You're nuts. You're upset. Don't say anything. My God. The people. Kids. Where's Quentie?" His collar open, his checked wool shirt with the striped green tie hanging down, staying three feet away from her, bending forward, soliciting. She put both hands in the air and started scratching it. A craziness he'd never seen. Her voice, trembling, was soft again, but full of the syllabic menace. "Please. Pull-e-a-s-e g-e-t o-u-t. O-u-t." The hands fell to the blanket, the head to the pillow. Edward rocked back and forth, his hand still up with the book, angry but not going.

Then a banging at the kitchen window, Cammie yelling something. "Mommie, Mommie," is all he got, and he said, "See, see what you've done? You fucking nut." Turning for the door, when WHAM, knocko, in his ear, his hand went up, what a blast. The shoe dropped on the carpet. He spun and threw the book into her stomach. She grunted, terribly, and then, more terribly, laughed. He slammed the door behind him and yelled, "It's nothing, Cammie. Be right there. Mommie just hit her leg against the bed," went to the front door and opened it. "Go back and play. Mamma's tired. It's her period. Here, get some chocolate at the *Tabacchi,*" getting a hundred-lire coin into her glove, smiling into the dark, bunched-up face.

He sat in the kitchen, listening to the fountain, gush, splash, brrr, gush, splash. Across the way a face. Olga's? Marisa's? One of the *tombolo* players? Looking. He nodded coldly, turned to the table, put his elbows on it. How could she have? She couldn't have. The most she could have was seeing us together arm in arm, but she knows we go around together, no harm there, or not much. Was there something in our faces? Or could she, no, we were in an alley, there was no one, I looked, the chances one in a million. Maybe Olga saw and told her, or Lydia walking with Quentin? No, they never went off the Giudecca.

Or she's just nuts.

No, she saw us, and deduced the rest. What to do? Time. No, get back, repentance, explanation. "You know what it's been like, Cressy. A man can't just go on air." Except that for a month that excuse didn't hold.

New Year's. She's heard about New Year's. Of course. The door wide open, the place full of sharks, Fogleman, Civita, any of them. McGowan. The Sniffer. He could sniff it a mile off. He'd spilled the beans.

He slammed the table, pain, bread-crust bits cutting the soft flat of his hand.

He went back to the room. She was crying. It was dark, except for the vortex of silky yellow light from his lamp. Cressida was barely an outline.

"Cress, I beg you. Forgive. You know the way it was with us. I held and held. And then something happened, for one second, and that was it. I was drunk. She was off her head. It was crazy. Imagine? A party. The door open." His hand in his hot ear, standing out of the light.

The sobs stopped. "I saw you today, Edward. Just today. Not at the party. Not God knows where else. Just today. I'm tired. I've had it. Let's call it off. Tonight. At least tonight. Go take supper in town. Take Brose and Cammie with you. Tell them I'm not feeling well."

He did not look at her. When he finished washing he came back, put on his coat and fixed his tie. "I'll put the light out, Cress. If I see Lydia, I'll tell her to give Quent his supper and put him to bed. I won't bother to explain. You know the way I am. But you, I hope you know how I care. I hope you'll. Etcetera. You know."

And left without looking at her, though not without hearing the sobbing, mocking, furious noise which constituted her response.

❧ chapter 12

And if you could manage, without of course altering Sir Georgie, to thin out the cheeks. It was the way he looked till the Jubilee.' 'Well,' I said, 'the stone's bought already, y'know, it means a bit of waste.' As it came out, he looked like the full moon crossed with a schnauzer. 'But you didn't trim Sir Georgie,' she'd see me in court before she'd give thruppence for it. 'And the hours Sir Georgie sat breathing stone dust in your—I suppose you call it a stew-dyo.' It looked as if I'd be in court paying Georgie thirty shillings an hour for those labors. Don't know where he reposes now. I think the South Kensington." Stroking the clay on the wire tangle. Hardly up to the T-bar under the cheeks let alone the tremble there. What had put those pinch marks in her face, pushed the forehead ledge toward the sockets? He couldn't soften her.

"After Jutland, I got a crown commission to do Fotheringby. Admiral. Gloomiest buzzard in England, but I thought I'd be set for a year. He wouldn't concede a 'Good morning.' He'd give me two sittings, though he didn't approve. For the Nation. One of the 'obligtry, auxlry ditties.' Had to ask him to remove his cap. He thought he wouldn't be recognized without it. Terrible face. Cherubic, with satanic lips. And side whiskers. Like Schubert's. He looked like a villainous Schubert. Would come in, nod, face the wall and stare. For two hours. 'Be all, I spose,' and off. The height of his civility. Last day I swabbed the chair with Number One glue. For two hours he didn't notice. Extraordinary sitter. When he got up, the chair rose with him. 'Dear me, Admiral,' said I. 'You seem to be running off with m'chair.' 'Year or two in the fleet would do you to a turn, Mister.' They got some Mayfair gravestoner to do him. So, you see, unlike Jacob, I didn't have the knack for making a thing of portraits. My total income in 1921 was two hundred dollars, thirty pounds, and eighty francs. I used to have the exact figure in my head. I considered putting it on my calling card."

But it was never only money. Her trouble was not that. Money only masked real troubles. His hands, humped with calcium ridges, messed around in the clay, fingers working in pairs, articulation clotted. Not that he needed hands for the island. Vision, knowledge, memory. The island was the only thing he had the war hadn't made superfluous. There was no more twitting the Fotheringbys, the Georgies. Their lies put hands on every throat. They'd killed a slue, Guillaume and Gaudier and T.E. So many killed, and so many others turned foolish. Even Henry. As if it were one flag or the other that dressed benevolence. Henry turning puppet. And like Whitman, turning nurse as well; mopping the spilled milk. But the puppeteer's business had to be our business. So the sessions over

Signor Rotamundi's pasta. And then, en route to see Jim in Trieste, the island. Waiting for him in the lagoon. And the flash had come, and he knew everything would be there. And he hadn't gone to Jim's.

Years his mind had swum in forms, eye skinned flesh from elementing forms: command's ellipsis, the droop and scatter of *l'homme moyen*. While haste, tantrums, vanity, lotus-gobbling, self-gratulation nibbled away. Dreaming beauty, waking with sluts.

On and on, eyes open. Without an Ithaca. Unlike Angelmike, he could not orate his way there. And now, the mind like flayed skin hung on rusted memory. Going through motions on the armature, unable to touch the interrogative sweetness of the cheek.

The first warm day in months. February? No, March. He hadn't been out of bed for four days, hadn't seen Nina for six. During which her face had altered with trouble. "What's wrong, Nina?" He kept his hands on the clay, fingers caressing more than forming. Her face rising from the sea-green fiber of her sweater.

The forehead uncorrugated under the child's straight hair.

"Mostly Nina," said Nina.

Not improbably. Low in impulse, sureness by exclusion. Like many women, Mary B., Gretta, some men, Sean—many Irishmen—Glauco—not many Italians. The women usually better than the men, able to work under the do-not-touch signs. Their passion for sea, mountains, high, void prospects. They collected things, cooked well, flirted, rarely bedded down, then "just to see," worked very hard. Yes, fine work could come. The human container was not greatly various but it allowed for this. Usually there were families, friends, high talk, and occasionally, confession. This one seemed alone. "The sun should be doing better in a few weeks. You'll get out. We'll walk. On the Lido to Alberoni, or out on Torcello."

"If I can hold out."

Well, it was also money. Where he couldn't help her. Aside from feeding her, and he assumed Bicci bore that burden. Joanna had his funds. Whatever the government let through. He didn't bother with it. The women took care of it. Maybe Camerino could get her something on the *Gazzettino*. Or why didn't she write "Letters from Italy" for the magazines? If she did two a month, it ought to see her through.

Lucia brought them tea, put a cup by the armature, another in Nina's hand. The steam showed in curve slats where the shutter barred the light. Nina's face softened. A Celt but no Boadicea, no Maud—poor Yeats's girl. Drinking, she did not purse her lips for the heat. The course of the tea in her mouth, her throat, even in her chest between the hidden breasts, fuller than in most women of low force. Tea. What would the form of tea be? Not a leaf form. Not a pot or cup. Maybe the small life of the throat as it swallowed, an expansion near the voice box as it signaled the Englishman it was time for his day's quota of lies. Two lifted throat parts, bulges, moving toward each other.

Yet tea worked, intrusion of hot liquidity altering sluggish balance. For five minutes after the initial swallow he was ready for the island. If the swallowing were transport, he had twenty or thirty strokes in him, and if he had tea twice a day for a year, this would be thirty thousand strokes and that could mean half a head. In ten years he'd have five heads.

No. There were to be no more heads, or only those very few

with whom he would wish to talk forever, some already there, Wolfgang, Donato, Naso, Frederick, Jeff, Kung. But here, now, that brown head regarding him over the wisp of steam? No, what was the point? He'd done all that fifty years ago, that Stitch who thought it a matter of sheer leverage to open the oyster, thought leverage itself made pearls. "That'll have to be it, Nina."

"Thank you," she said. "It's really coming along."

2

When she'd come back after supper last night, there'd been a note from Countess Lustraferri: "Please immediately at your own suitability to see me." The first communication since the initial visit with the Baron, except for a few "Buon giornos" in the hall. It must mean the roof was really falling in. She hadn't made one rental payment. She should have made one early to calk the amnesiac sieve. After all, the woman wouldn't be renting at all unless she needed money. The heat and electricity bills went to her. Even the most sluggish would know substance was diminishing, not augmenting. And who knows if the woman hadn't been jarred by what happened with Edward? They had surely made noise, at least on the stairs, and that two hundred pounds plus her own hundred and ten drew God knows what noises from bed to walls. The Countess should surely not frown on anything after the Baron, but maybe her sea of vagueness contained only the wreck of young women. Her own wreck. Who knows? It could be the one intolerable, memory-stimulating event.

Nina, the housewrecker.

What was happening to her? Emily Dickinson had stayed home. Jane Austen had stayed home. Sappho was well-off. Louise Labé, Anna Akhmatova, Hrotswitha, Christine Pisan had their troubles, but money? No. *Le mal que j'ai, et tu le ses, Argent.* When you had troubles, you were a troublemaker. When you were a troublemaker, you kept making trouble.

She and Stitch and Edward. All in their season made trouble. Stitch, thinking the state could carve life, Edward, thinking life was a room in a museum. And she, little Moll Flanders, turned into a Venetian character by, well, by men and mazooma. A failure of the parts and maybe of the whole, the long plan gummed up, rotting along with the billion other defective plans which annually yielded to winter.

Hold it, Nina. There's a double line to perspective, the here and now, and the over-all. Any mistaking one for the other means distortion. The here and now is Lustraferri. Delaying, conning, or better, paying. It has to be done. Maybe a month's rent, even two, and then a little line with it, cheese plus sweet talk. "Sorry I've forgotten since the New Year, Contessa." But the cheese. Where, whom? Edward. But twice, she'd really be Moll, a flesh merchant. And besides, this time, almost, yes, there'd been something not to be traded.

There had to be things to trade.

She surveyed the room, the hanging wash, the filled shelves, the quilted bed she sat on.

Books?

No, she could not part with what kept her above water. And there weren't enough for what she needed.

Clothes?

Yes, better. Where did you sell clothes in Venice? The Mount of Piety would not do well by her ratty fur. Who was her size, and who, that had the money to buy, wouldn't buy their own? Fogleman? No. If it meant pulling a human being out of the drink, she lost interest. Maybe some fruit who liked to dress up in his room at night. The list was endless, but she knew none well enough to raise the possibility. "Thought your mother would like to take this off my hands."

If she had Charley, he would go for twenty thousand. Even Fogleman might buy him.

She came to the little bronze centaur, the desk's sole ornament, the room's beauty.

This might do it.

Stitch would understand. He'd known what it was like to be up the creek. It would go for plenty, maybe three hundred bucks. Fogleman would snatch it up if she believed Nina didn't need the money. "I'm tired of the damn thing, I want to buy one of his big heads, Mrs. F. I feel guilty about the other night, so I thought I'd offer it to you instead of the museum."

But Lord God. Why should such a one own anything made with love and genius? Stitch wouldn't like that. No, she could not sell it; it was a need.

She went to sleep, trusting night to come up with an answer.

But daylight swept the floor through the French doors, and Nina was blank. In the hall she heard some odd scraping noise. "God. Lustraferri. She's coming." No, the Countess wouldn't descend for such a summons. Venetians didn't hurry.

She'd take the morning to think things out and go see her after lunch. She reached from her bed and put her hand on the little bronze body. Not this.

When she got back from Stitch's and a bowl of *zuppa di pomidoro* at Bicci's, she'd made up her mind to face it out directly: "I've got nothing, Countess. Nothing in the world. Hardly a hope. I fall on my hands. It's up to you. Throw me out. I'll understand." And she went upstairs, practicing it.

The Countess, in her fuchsia dressing gown, opened the door herself, her large powdered nose pushed out through stray flops of red hair. "Ah, *sì, sì, sì, Signorina, cara.* Yes, am so happy. Come right in, take it, I've keeped it all night. A darling. Look," and pulled Nina by the arm to a white and gold couch on which, ensconced over a large bone embraced by his jaws, was a brown and white tube with a long, trembling muzzle. Trembling spread over the tube as if it were filled with striped jelly. "The big American carried it yesterday night. Could not took it home, he said, he must leave it, would I give it between you? *Tanto carino, non? Sì, caro. Caro,*" and the Countess buried the little dog—now yelping in a tiny voice, like jelly's squiggle —in fuchsia.

Nina's heart spread with joy. So, this was it. No bills, no call to beg, to act Raskolnikov. A *hundchen* from Eddy. No Charley, only a miserable little trembler, but what a kindness. What a decent thing.

The Countess insisted on frequent visits from the *piccolino.* "I shall held the divan for him," she said, touching the abandoned white and gold couch soiled deeply now with the quiverer's response to love. Nina envisaged a new source of funds. It compensated for the training hours ahead.

3

Edward showed up ten minutes after Nina had gotten Carlo to recognize the shag rug as his bed and the adjacent *Gazzettino* as his toilet. It was going to be a long struggle, for this creature was born to fear and his sole response to the world's loud syllables was his pitiful trickle of urine. Contempt and pity mixed with Nina's loneliness, and she took him in more as project than companion. Edward, who came upstairs carrying a plaid overnight bag, roused small yelps of terror. Nina put her arms around his shoulders. "You did a sweet thing, lover. Where'd you get'm?"

"Campo S. M. Formosa. I had the kids out for supper last night—tell you about it—and they spotted him on sale with six siblings. What's his name?"

"Carlo Marx," said Nina. "He comes in a time of material crisis, so I look to him for solution."

"I've got a better solution."

He sat on the bed beside Nina, his face splotched with red and white strain signs. The troublemakers were apparently having their troubles all over. "What is it?"

"Take a trip with me. I called Nol-Auto and there's a Seicento on its way over to Piazzale Roma from Mestre. It'll be there by the time our boat gets there. Throw a few things in a bag and we'll take a little tour. On me. The works."

"This have something to do with your supper in town?"

He lay back on the bed, torso circling her body, face against her skirted thigh. "She saw us." Nina was up like a shot. A yelp shimmied out of Carlo followed by a trickle into the rug.

Edward raised himself, reached for her hand, which moved out of reach. Oh no, not again. He forced himself through the chill. "Walking, or I guess running and holding hands or arm in arm or something, yesterday."

Whirl. "What's that mean? Nothing! I thought she *saw* us. There's something omitted." She crouched to cat shape, skirling

[132]

terror from the miserable Carlo, looked into Edward's flushing face, and spoke fiercely. "You told her. You opened up. Confessional. What are you trying to do? Huh? The two of you? What are you trying to do to me?"

"To you?" He slapped his palms around her arms below the shoulders. "What in hell have you got to lose on heaven or earth? I've got children she can take from me. You? What's it matter to you what anyone thinks? Where the hell does your reputation suffer? You're down to the floor right now. You can't go one inch lower."

So that's the way they turned. Yes, when the heat went up a half degree. The burgher-adulterers. These quick condemners. Shake them one inch from their fixity, touch them with one crystal of snow, and they turn wolf. Howling tuns of flesh, consuming villages' worth of stuff, the world sweating for their ease. And now, doubled back on their own pleasures, the cornucopia stuffed so the seams strained, they turned wolf.

He hadn't stopped. "You with your grand excuse. You think 'cause you can tinkle a couple of words together it gives you open season all year long. On anybody or anything. Some gift to the world. You and that old beard. He turned round and spit at everything which gave him his fur-lined pulpit for thirty years. 'Cause he can bash a piece-uh rock he's got a pass to bash six million Jews like lice. And you. Nothing matters but your—your *what?* You haven't even got the what yet."

Yes, now the Jew bit. Poor, defenseless fellow. Reserving his place in the ovens. I can see him making deals with the gauleiters, rounding up the peddlers and baby momsers. No limit for these lice. They date the beginning and the end of things with last week. And talks about me. His face white

[133]

now, under the steak. Flushing. Hands on me. Foundation's the tongue. Brain like Carlo's bladder.

She hunched shoulders, gathering for a break from his grip, and then, even as his fingers felt the muscles humping, she shot a hand at his head and caressed it, cheek, hair, lips. After all. "Absurd. This is nuts, Eddy. Come on. We're not in a soap opera. Let's make sense of it. Forgive me. Look, poor Carlo hasn't a drop to spare," and they regarded the striped quiverer burrowing into the graying shag. Edward drew Nina's head toward him and rubbed her cheek with his.

And rubbing, confessed. "Forgive me, Nina. My tongue. Just like with Cressida. I talked before I knew what I was doing. Sure, I let it out about us. She saw us walking, yes, but I thought someone had told her about New Year's Eve. I said we were drunk, out of our heads. Forgive me. She threw a shoe at me. Hit me. She went out of her head. Like me now. What's to become of us?"

Who was "us"? "Easy now, Eddy. It's O.K. I'll just steer clear. She must think it's Circe's cave down here. Some seductress. Oh, Lord," with a laryngeal growl-groan he felt in his own face. "No, no, don't fool," moving away from face, hand. "The trip. Where?"

"All right, yes, the trip," and shook himself out. "Down the coast. Padua, Ferrara, Ravenna, Rimini, maybe Urbino, Arezzo, Firenze, Siena, down to Rome. We could even make it all the way down the toe. Sicily. Not quite. The kids. I can't leave them too long. And your work. You don't ... You know I think you're a wonderful poet. You know how I believe in all that."

"*Non fa nulla.*" She stooped for the exhausted Carlo. "But I can't go with old Carlo. You've sweetened my life with him. I can't desert him the first day. And we can't take him."

" 'Sno trouble. In the back seat."

"Peeing on your shirts."

"The Countess. She seemed to like him."

"No," said Nina. "She said no. She's got dust-fever. Like hay-fever. From dogs. It was O.K. last night, but not for long. No, I can't make it. You'll have a better time this way. No diversions. We'll forget the big speeches. You were great to give me Carlo. That's what counts. Not the edge of your tongue. You go. We'd just be getting tangled up if we went together."

And when he was off on the *accelerato* to Piazzale Roma, waving to her from the back rail, a brown campanile with a green turret, she extracted Carlo from her coat and held him up in one hand for farewell. "Say 'By-by, Pop,' " and then hustled this trembling product of her time with Edward into her coat along with the 10,000-lire note with which he'd bought off his tirade. Carlo would understand that. "Don't wet your blood money, Carlo. It's all for you." Leash, coat, food. Even the generosity of troublemakers brought trouble.

She decided to go in Santa Maria del Giglio with Carlo. There'd be no one there now. She needed quiet, serious quiet. But it was ten minutes shy of four; the doors were locked. The need wasn't worth the wait or the walk to San Marco. She asked in the antique store in the calle for a piece of rope. Fixed to a piece of cloth on Carlo's neck, it would be a good enough leash; she could contrive a garment out of one of her pockets. She still owed Charley's butcher for bones, so she tried the Macellaio Gabrielli in Campo Sant' Angelo and walked off with two bones and some pig liver. Edward would be driving along the Brenta now, past the shuttered villas, *Malcontenta, Schifanoia, Melancholia,* Palladian evasions like

his own, unavailable to the poor, the be-dogged. Well and good.
She and Carlo were on their own. A premonition of warmth
hovered in the chill, the world lay ready to be metered, she was
fed, housed, companioned, her body had known passion, her
mind was not tangled in it, she'd reached the bottom of poetic
miseries, there was no place to go but upward. "Ywill have
my world as in my tyme," she sang beneath her lips, the line
almost visible to her amidst the jewel-knobbed fretwork trilobed
on palace brick. The Wyf of Bath and Nina, the sisterhood,
only one of which was so far carved upon the world, and that
by masculine hands. Yea, Carlo, we-uns shall cut our little
selves into the world before long. Thee and me.

❧ chapter 13

It is in the high noon of Augustan civility that ~~one of Augustus~~ Quintus Horatius Flaccus sings of the incapacity of nature ~~did not~~ to distinguish right from wrong. ~~that~~ Justice, he ~~sings~~ points out, is the human invention which defends its inventors against ~~natural~~ nature's injustice.

Two unmillennial millennia afterwards in a more comprehensive ~~if less intense~~ intensive civility, uncapitalized nature is the Other from which (not whom) inventors crib not order but insight. When convention matches nature, happiness comes. This is the axiom of the author of the ~~Philosophical Dictionary~~ Dictionaire Philosophique. (sp?) The misty balance of crossed force whose larger interruptions are the consciousness of the honorable species of whom I am one, is the court of ultimate appeal, ~~lying~~ ready beyond even the double helix whose ten trillion units of information form this great interruption. The inorganic seat of consciousness may, who knows, turn out to be a larger form of consciousness, tappable by the smaller. What transfiguration of our condition this would be. Meanwhile, back with ~~Quintus Hor~~ Horace, back with the great figures, named and anonymous, whose

[137]

words, pigments, traditions, stones are the earthly ideal which
until we pierce the mist of force must guide, provoke, judge us.

S O EDWARD'S NEW ESSAY ENDS. It is something for
him, and he holds the typed sheets in fingers so sensitively
agitated by the fatigue of typing and the excitement of release
that he can almost feel the prickle of the black letters under
his fingertips. He cannot wait to read it, to Cressida, to Nina,
maybe to Stitch. With it and the siblings he has been engen-
dering for a month, he joins the world's producers. He sits at
an immense desk by velvet curtains, the door closed against
the invasions of his own dear Quintus. Four months left in
their year—though perhaps they will stay longer—and the door
has opened for him. Has he at last found the harbor for which
he'd left Chicago?

He slides the yellow pages into the top drawer of the desk
upon their older brothers. When there are two hundred sheets,
he will reread, reorder, connect them with each other, and then
spring them full-grown onto Nina. With her approval, he
will send them to a publisher, or to literary and philosophical
quarterlies.

Though perhaps he should expand more, write on a greater
variety of subjects so that his Acknowledgments page will indi-
cate ubiquitous expertise, thus subdue the brutal confidence
of reviewers and succeed in getting him reviewed in a variety
of journals, *Art Bulletin, Daedalus, Ethics, The Journal of the*

History of Ideas. The amateur scholar, the Emersonian ideal. They are few and far between. The usual commentators were professional writers, editors, professors, loaded with vested interest, competing with each other at New York parties, maneuvering for university posts, damning pieces in which their names could have appeared and didn't. Where were the new Thoreaus? There was some laborer out on the West Coast, but he was probably a phony cracker-barreler. Now and then a man left his domain to write on something conspicuously remote from it, but where was the true floating intelligence, above issues, in touch with the past and the best of the two cultures? A slot gaped for him. The combination of his public relations—foundation gifts and his speculative power could even lead to popular attention. He would give an occasional lecture tour, first at universities, then to the Rand Corporation, the Georgetown University Seminars, the War Colleges. There would be international conferences under the auspices of the Congress for Cultural Freedom, and he would cross an occasional sword with Jouvenel, Lukács, Aron, Madariaga, Polanyi, Shils. There couldn't be much difference between such minds and his own. Once he developed the habit of application. Whatever arose one examined and located in the galaxy of one's knowledge. Everything counted, newspaper items, statues, family quarrels. The same principles applied to stars and feelings. Emotions were referred to the heart to keep up the link with matter. The chemistry of emotions existed now. When Quentin had children, there would be a physics of emotion, there would be an emotion of matter. The sun's in love, the earth's in pain. Swedenborg. He touched one of the unused yellow sheets. This pile was diminishing. No, he was tired now, he had to discipline himself. One essay a day was enough. The stream would run dry. Discipline meant daily work. Besides, it was time to switch fields. He'd been too abstract. It was time to examine human relations. Atomically. As if they'd never before been considered. What are the physical manifestations of a quarrel? Is a quarrel related to a new matter or an old? No, this was familiar. And the debate between Cannon and James about bodily changes in fear and pain probably went back to the Middle Ages. Did throat constriction cause fear or fear throat constriction? Or was it different in each age? Take McCluhan's views about ages of print, ages of manuscript, automobile and electric ages. The dominant media change the nature of social organizations, architecture, thought patterns, behavior. Perhaps in a walled city, remote from central control, the common man's connection with culture came only in his speech, his role in ritual, obedience to what he'd been taught to deem universal, the . . . the what? Where was he? Ideas. Cannon. Emotion. The emotion is dominant. Or rather, with primitive man, energy. Quick to anger, quick to love, quick to respond in a few crude ways to the few discriminated stimuli. Whereas, yes, in a time of enormous data, where every sense was flooded with something to categorize, energy was cerebral, emotions confused; people were troubled by blockage in the categorizing faculties and moved quickly to the psychiatrist or to sex. Perhaps analysis would help. No. He'd never felt that need. But perhaps he could live more temperately. No. He was temperate. It was Cress who'd been intemperate. Negatively. Steps were missing. There was something there. But wait.

Edward went to his bed, put the pillow around his ears,

closed his eyes in proudly earned fatigue. A data-clotted product. He lay there until he heard the mailman shouting *"Poste, Goon-tair."* then sprang up with his lifetime's trust in the fecundity of mail and found nothing but the W-2 forms from his five 1962 Noonan months. It set him off, heart raging, to pick up tax forms from the consulate.

2

The essays were not forgotten though, even in the uproar of the next two days. Crossing the canal with Brose and Cammie the night of Cressida's outbreak—rubbing his ear where it ached from her shoe—he tried to cure the steaming wound with analytic ice. The factors: Cress's yearlong fatigue, her period coming on, her envy of his leisure, her thinking it was coming to an end and then seeing him cavorting around, and then worse, hearing drastic confirmation she hadn't known about. Then, too, the dark of the room, the cold house, and, God knows, himself. To describe all this coolly in terms of the twentieth-century family, marriage of Jew and Gentile, the second-chance American getting ready for a third chance, the uneducated midwestern girl in vertical mobility (marriage with an intellectual), the American in Europe, *Gemeinschaft* exposed to *Gesellschaft,* all this against the loves and woes of the flesh. Yes, there was a great little history that could be written if he would keep cool and think it out.

The essays weren't forgotten as he decided to take the trip the next day. He'd watched Brose and Cammie running off in their black smocks to catch the 8:29 vaporetto, blown kisses at their backs, and gone into the kitchen for his coffee. Quentin in his blue sleepers on a high chair lopping up Corn Flakes, interrupted the devotions for Daddy's kiss.

Cressida stood by the window, regarding the courtyard, or perhaps the courtyard wall which gathered enough weak sun for its morning's rosy shower. She was in her red bathrobe, furry loafers, wool socks.

"Coffee ready?"

"On the stove," without turning toward him. Her hair, tied back in a bun, her back straight, emphasizing the squareness of the shoulders. Yes, thought Edward, there's a streak of man in her. Repressed assertiveness. She winged that shoe like Willie Mays. He poured the coffee from the yellow-flowered Swedish maker into one of the plump white cups, scooped in three spoonfuls of sugar, and sat across from Quentin. "Had yours yet?"

"Huh?" from Quentin.

"Eat your cereal. I'm talking to Mommie."

"Huh?"

"Any rolls?"

She pointed to the breadbox, got butter from the refrigerator, and slid it to him across the table. Quentin dripped with softened flakes; Cressida lifted him down and told him to see if Lydia was coming.

"I think the best thing would be for me to go away for a few days." A brief smile of contempt, the like of which he'd not seen on her face for weeks. At least I can affect her somehow. "Just for three or four days. I've got something I might write about. And it would cool this situation off."

"Suit yourself. Of course that's advice you're not in need of."

"Cress, either we're going to live together or we're not. What

[142]

kind of nonsense is this? You know I'm almost pathetically virtuous. I mean in the old-fashioned way. We've been under months of strain. I reacted. Drunk and disorderly. That's no lifetime sentence."

"You never understand." She poured herself coffee and stood by the stove drinking it. She did not clarify.

"I'm afraid I don't."

"Never mind." What had "mind" to do with it?

He packed his bag looking away from her as she dressed; he must not be derailed. When he left, she was in the courtyard talking to Signora Marisa. "Good-by, Cress," he called from the staircase. She looked up and said, "Good-by."

From the tunneled doorway he turned and waved, but she was facing Signora Marisa and didn't see him. He dipped his gloved hand in the fountain, touched the cold water to his eyes and then walked toward the pier. Quentin was outside with Lydia, walking up the fondamenta wrapped in red earmuffs, his hands in fat brown mittens, his little blue coat down to his knees where navy blue pants were tucked into white rubber boots. Lydia pointed out "Papa" to him, removed his pacifier and started waving his little arm until recognition took over on its own. Quent stumbled toward Edward, who ran out to scoop up the dearest twenty pounds of his life, put his own shaven cheek next to the sweet softness of the baby's, kissed his eyes, ears, and—discarding sanitary fears, pushing down the mouth-high muffler—the tiny, full, damp lips. Like kissing a soul. He held him till the vaporetto pulled out of San Giorgio, and waved to the *Ciao*-waving baby from the open stern until he was again a point. What adoration he felt. It was an awful wrench, departing even for a day, going God knows how far

from children's accidents: falling into canals or the fondamenta's tide-worked holes, running into the heated grill of the
stove. Throughout his trip, he would feel the hook of love,
for Quentin, for the sweet, dark Cammie—so worried about
his arguments with Cressida—for hounded Brose, for the beauteous, betrayed femme, so cold in her bafflement, for—as the
boat turned the corner where the Mill stood and he lost sight
of it—the Giudecca, this cold, pathetic, intrepid little collection
of flaking, injured beauties.

3

In the Fiat the slush of fear and love solidified into his habitual
road anxieties. His hands sweated on the wheel, his nerves
bunched to pass a truck. Every five minutes he checked the
kilometrage against his expectations, Padova by eleven, lunch
in Ferrara, Ravenna before the churches closed at 3:30.

By the time he passed Rovigo on the way to Ferrara he decided Ravenna was too important to monopolize. He'd take
Cress and the children when it got warmer. They must not be
deprived of the mosaics. At Ferrara he'd turn off for Bologna,
drive as far as he felt, maybe to Pistoia, maybe Florence or
Siena, then go on to Rome tomorrow. Happiness was a combination of nostalgia and novelty. Rome had plenty for him.
For one thing, it had Sibyl, the beauty whom he had finally
hatched at Cuma.

In Bologna, after a look at San Petronio, he treated himself
to lunch at Pappagallo's and read the tourist pamphlets on the
city. Which delayed him an hour, as he had to see the double-
starred sights, but by 2:30 he was back on the Autostrada,
happy that Bologna was under his belt.

Two days later, he and Sibyl sat on the Aventine wall next to San' Saba looking down at the mud-yellow loops of the river sandwiched by walls and domes. Remains of their picnic—a bottle of Frascati, slices of ham and cheese, black olives, bread —scattered around them. Like the man-in-the-street's dream, thought Edward, whose pleasure declined from this insight.

"The Synagogue and St. Peter's look like the big shots from here," she said. "Like us."

"Some perspective. It's that dome there," said Edward, pointing to one flooded with silver that looked like a swollen biretta. "San Giovanni dei Fiorentini. Where they threw Lucrezia Borgia's first husband into the Tiber."

Smoke, drift, the towers seamed with silver and gold, the inescapable dome, a creamy, pink breast, coldly extended to cold sun. Talk, a billow of smoke domes, the transient presence, and then pssst. No solidity. The sun all dazzle, no heat, its light calling attention to itself. Below, a disheveled nag pulling a tourist carriage, cloppa, cloppa. Rome. He'd made the wrong turn. He should be sitting in dark Ravenna, garnering wisdom from the mosaics for his essays. Byzantium and the glass industry. Moslem shipping cutting it off in the seventh, no more mosaics till the eleventh; Sicily. Papyrus cut off from Egypt. Rome falls. Byzantium carries on with parchment. Twelfth century, paper from China: the twelfth-century renaissance. "Where there's smoke there's fire."

Sibyl drank, tilting the bottle. The grooves of her throat sank toward her chest, and Edward stared into her coat for what he had not seen since Cuma. Riverbeds of Frascati ran down his own.

"There's just too much," said Sibyl.

"We'll throw it away. No great waste."

"I mean our few troubles. Luxury troubles. We have too much. Isn't it so, Eddy?"

"I've tried that on. There's nothing to do about it. It just won't fit."

"It's unfair," she said. "Why should our lives take up so much room? Look over here. Just from here, millions grinding away so we can sit up here like kings."

Edward jerked his thumb at the creamy, corpulent church. "It's why these were started. All the religions, even the atheistic ones, Buddha, Confucius. To rescue the miserable. By making them dirt along with the rich."

"But what to do now? What good are they doing? You've got to be in condition to hear the message, Eddy."

"The churches are only a chapter. Rome's another chapter. We're all dots in the sweep of things. Individual effort's absurd. Look. The Khazars bust out in the east and knock the Lombards into Italy. The Franks move into Frankland. Martel needs money, confiscates church lands to maintain a cavalry, and so his grandson drives in and knocks the Lombards for a loop in Italy and gets crowned by the Pope right over there," thumb back at St. Peter's. "The big sweep. Hundreds of years. Where does that leave one man or ten? And it's only a paragraph. A tribe agitated by bad crops here, a gadget there. Who can tell what'll count? Louis the Fourteenth wins an argument about the windows at Versailles, so the builder loses his general's job, and the French lose in Holland so you get a Dutch king of England. Where does that put Jack and Jill? Sibyl and Eddy? Cavendish endows a laboratory, Rutherford is picked out of a hat, and fifty years later a hundred thousand people get turned to smoke at Hiroshima.

What can a man do? Look at my miserable life. Public relations man for a nut. We peddle chicken feed with a cold serum, then lose our shirts advertising in the summer when the chicks are all out in the sun. A perfumed insect destroyer, a no-bar hair curler. Where do they fit into things? I don't give a nickel to charity. I tell myself the rich get away with murder, it's their job to fix things up or let revolutions turn them out. Private lives. We're dots. Even thinking this is a luxury thought: the man with schooling enough to have opinions. What should I do? Work for Sncc, Snof and Core? Sure. Teach reading in the Congo? Better. Adopt a couple of orphaned Koreans? Shoot up the Pentagon? Better yet. And then what? Oil pops up in Yemen, they invent something in Schenectady, the biological warfare labs blow up, garbage chokes the rivers, and the sun dries out the Irish potato fields, anything, anywhere, and the world is topsy-turvy. What's a life in all this?"

"Still, still," and the face above the red tweed shakes in confusion, the blue eyes are chipped crystals of puzzled sympathy. "Each does his small bit. That's all. Instead of taking up so much room, time, money."

"Oh, Sib, God knows what enables us to sit up here and think big thoughts and drink in peace and have a little money in our pockets and you to look so beautiful and be so well."

"Eddy, what are we?"

"Who cares, Sib? Wine, you, and a view. No worry. No abstractions. Those who hog the world talk most abstractly about it. Napoleon said politics was invented to take the place of fate. Which only meant, 'I'm God, and don't try and stop me.' That's not for us, Sib. I don't think of you abstractly, Sib. Hegel said this place," waving at the silvered domes, the dazzled roofs, "was the great abstract power. Planning, codes, law. That's Rome. Not the inner man, ripening under the sun. Our feelings aren't stealing bread from down there."

He felt marvelous again. The Hegel had bubbled up from years back. At certain moments everything came to hand. This girl was made to be his. Open, educable, unrancorous, a beauty. A little too young but what did that count? That was abstraction. He loved this city, this girl, Italy, his own puzzlement, his own useless, granular life. Precious life, that so muddled a portion of it could contain such thoughts, such pleasures. Oh, you groaning commentators, loud-mouthed worriers, relax, rest, be pure, let time take you where it will. No more ambition, that clawing stupidity. No more hiding, disguising. Make the grain of things your own. Honesty is therapy. A smile uses fewer muscles than a frown. Listen to little Eddy, Sibyl. He was in her arms. Sibyl, Rome. So odorous, fruit-smelling, warm, soft, lips and tongue so full of love. Sibyl.

4

Two days later, Edward is driving from Rimini to Ravenna, his heart crying out his love for the cold sun, Italy, Europe, the world, Sibyl, Nina, Cressida, the children, but keeping a sharp eye for the Rubicon whose crossing—though south to north— he wishes to commemorate with his Baby Brownie as, two days before, he had commemorated himself and Sibyl, holding the box at arm's range and aiming it back at their heads twinned before the lantern of the Sapienza which, minutes before, had observed them embracing in the Hotel Bologna's *matrimoniale*. It is a brilliant day, the hills are turning, the farmers carve them into terraces with oxen. In Urbino, where he has spent the night after his last night with Sibyl, he had the harsh thought that he should not have left, that he has, thereby, said farewell to more than Sibyl, to possibility, open doors, youth, that his life, one way or another, is no longer physical, that his begotten children and half, maybe misbegotten, essays are his surrogates. But in the black Seicento, this insect hearse, he has reeled with the beauty of the fields, flowers, the Adriatic peeping through the rosy villas of Cattolica, the beautiful marble nymphs of Malatesta's temple, the straight blacktop road to Ravenna. Movement, change—his old gods—here in the sun, flight-free—nests in Rome, Venice, Chicago, with, who knows, Santa Barbara coming up—gathering in joy's honeycomb the sweet material of his commentaries, he is, within the snug Six Hundred, Zeus en route, a speeding power, ready to take any form, bull, golden rain, movie producer, whatever the hour demands.

Oh, Sibyl, thank you, my beauty. Oh, Italy, thank you, my love.

He drives under a blue banner with red lettering, VOTA PCI, then, nerveless, unsweating, maneuvers in and out of a line of tanker trucks and enters the pink and mocha center of Ravenna.

An hour later, under the rainbow boiling out of the dark gold mosaics of the memorial to Galla Placidia, he says out loud, "Holy Jesus, I forgot." The Rubicon.

❧ chapter 14

Hᴇʀ ʟɪꜰᴇ had to play a role, certainly. What she
had seen, noted, what had counted for her. But whatever went
in would be placed in her map of the transient, the immu-
table, and the reborn. Aquinas' blueprint was no longer
useful. Nor was Troy, nor any history. Her palette would
include the epic writers' strategies, mutation from Ovid, the
voyage from Homer, the home-away-from-home cosmos of
Hesiod, the meetings of gods and men from Gilgamesh to
Joyce, none would dominate. As for the actors, they'd be
arranged in series, Aeneas, the pious, swindling founder, Augustus, the ironic commissioner, Vergil, the lyric scribe broken
by state service, Dante, the noble pupil, Milton, Camoëns, and
the Beowulfer, the stuffy, ambitious imitators. And prophets,
scholars, heroes, loud and soft, Francis L. next to Carolus
Magnus, Stitch beside Arjuna. And the muckers, two-for-
oners, parasites, finaglers, Civitas, Savonarolas, Foglemans and
Fuggers.

Under her dripping underwear, above Carlo, yapping and urinating at the canal noises from the open window, Nina began. Not with the little purgatorial boat which hadn't made it out of the harbor New Year's Eve, but with her sisters, human, divine, and mixed, the givers of songs and children, the consolers, continuers, the makers of homes to which heroes returned, the vessels of civility, transmitters of culture, the mothers of the gods.

Nymphs swam in the trees, branched in the waters; old women and forsaken wives wove and knitted; girls like rosy balls of fruit tempted gods and men.

Music ran through Nina. Time dissolved in it, words formed in it.

Her underwear dripped on the white paper, blotting. Light faded. Nina wrote as if played by a giant.

In the dark she stopped, fed Carlo, folded her clothes, ate bread—staler each day—and cheese—moldier and sweeter— lit the lamp and went on until sleep blotted her mind. In the morning, she got up, dressed in the same clothes in which, the day before, she'd said good-by to Edward, and took up where she'd left off.

So it went for four days. She lived on the inner music, did not leave the apartment—it reeked of Carlo's functions— ate but crackers, the staling bread, the rotting cheese, did not go downstairs once, slept but twelve hours in the four days.

On the fifth day the music stopped; the giant had finished. Nina went to bed dressed in the same skirt and sweater, and slept from 10:30 in the morning to nine that night, woke up in a panic of hunger, her head reeling with the smell and filth of the room, threw up in the toilet, went to a bar, ate three ham sandwiches and drank two tumblers of Vecchia Romagna. She went back and cleaned her place in a fury till one o'clock, gave the half-dead Carlo a bath and a bone, and slept till ten the next morning.

❧ chapter 15

For this first spring day Stitch wore a tan cape, fixed at the neckline with velveted clips, and a huge-brimmed Italian priest's hat. On the boat he said nothing. Ten minutes before they reached Sant' Ilario he took Nina's hand and held it till they pulled into the quay.

Again they were the only visitors. On the path up the just-greening hill he took the picnic basket from Nina and swung with it, his step lighter, less flat, the toes straight ahead. He was fifteen years younger in this weather.

The idea of the excursion had been Miss Fry's. For the first time this year she had begun to disbelieve in the inexhaustibility of his energy, but she had not lived nearly forty years with him to discard revival. And since his old bursts of power had always been connected with women, with her, with Joanna, with many others, why not now, in some fashion anyway, with Nina?

Thus the picnic basket with the gold wine of Genoa and

soft capon, the sun, the pretty little scrapper, and his island. The girl had brought her new poem, the beginning of an epic, and he was going to do as well as a man could who was thirty years behind the times, listen as hard as he could, and hope by that to make up a little for not knowing what the lay of the poetic land was.

Though he could not imagine it was time for another epic. Discounting his own version, which, as far as carving went, was the first one-man job since Gislebertus carved St. Lazaire, there was still Proust. As a sculptor, he'd not felt the shadow-chill that work had cast on all his epic-minded friends. Jim and Ezra had refused to read more than a few pages. And done well not to. Conrad and Henry had saluted it, but they'd not had the packaging ambition. *La pauvre* Gide had tried to stifle it at birth.

The epic of temperament, as Dante's was of belief and Homer's of body. He'd seen its Homer only once. Where? At Noailles or at some Hebrew bluestocking's. Wearing a fur coat in the salon, a rickety Sloterman, the flesh sensitive as an eye. Yet a Newton. The eye as spine, brain. That holy power of recollection. And muscle. A man who knew Sancho's belly had busted Venus' girdle.

Did this one?

Give her an uncomparisoned ear. You can't fornicate with someone else's.

He knew where what amounted to a seat was, a bow of tremolite, green more than gray because of the iron wash. He'd found it in the Vaud when he'd driven up with Joanna and Hem, and she'd gotten jaundice and he'd worked it there and shipped it back in April, twenty-eight years next month. Bole as well as bow, it worked itself into sea nymphs as in the Miracoli. He'd taken naps there five hundred times.

"Why don't you read a bit now, Nina?"

She was ready, anxious. Not wholly out of her trance, she could still feel the extraordinary force of his attention, a hot light, without remission, yet patient. Sitting beside him on the stone couch, she read.

Her work was a horse beneath her. She knew its pace, its power. Exhibition, not performance. There it was, what she knew, thought, felt. The convocation of the great, the incarnations, air alive with transmission, the large scene broken into the new music. Sappho, Christine de Pisan, Louise de Lyons, the Countess of Die, Anne of Byzantium, Jane of England, Colette of France, Emily of Amherst, Sor Juana de Mexique, her sisters, singing with her. Conception, womb, the ripening of gentility, amenity, warmth, manners, custom, the domestication of cosmos.

She read for an hour. When she stopped, voice husky, Stitch unfolded himself and walked, rigidly, in his maze, disappearing behind a low relief of Assyrian bulls, reappearing higher up beside what appeared both coupling doves and alabaster whirlpool. From there he looked down at her. She smiled up, a bulldog's smile. His eyes, between alabaster feathers, gleamed, remote, ferocious, skeptic. She folded the manuscript into her purse and opened the basket. "Lost your appetite?"

Back behind the relief and then off on another tack near a banquet table with heads, some clear, some fouled by other forms like fused double births. Maybe, thought Nina, he thinks he's been displaced. Instead of reviving him, pleasing him, she'd only thrown down the gauntlet of the new, come knocking at the door to carry him off in the coffin. Perhaps he couldn't follow her and was now wandering in his own maze getting back self-confidence.

But why? Theirs was the same enterprise. Surely he saw that. His was further out than her own, but neither had made endearing gestures for the crowd. They were brother and sister. Had her song deranged that?

He was as high as his own work permitted now, standing on a kind of regal coxcomb, his back to her, facing the city over the lagoon. A jot of gold from the Campanile gleamed by the gray head.

Remoteness? Francis L. had the same sort. There to raise and judge them, not be treated to their accomplishments. Presenting them to the world. But she was not his and not Stitch's.

She drove in the corkscrew, drew the cork out with a jerk and poured the pale gold into two glasses. He was beside her, hand on her hair. "Much good there. I can see you're getting at something." He took up a glass. "Here's to it, Nina."

It was something. "Can you see your way clear in it?"

"Pretty much."

"But . . ."

"Yes, 'but,' and the 'but' may be in me, Nina. I know nothing for sure. It felt like a good, clear draught. Tough-minded, musical, alive, marked with your knowledge, your restlessness, your curiosity."

This was something more, but Nina knew it was now less than before he'd said anything, his head beside the gold jot of the Campanile. He had praised it as a piece, *sui generis,* but he was seeing her now in that long run which was the only one that counted—even in the short run. There was the great matter and manner, or there wasn't. One discovered or one did not. One added or one did not. One sowed and harvested, or consumed other men's work. Makers or servers: this was the division of artists.

"I think you have it. Inside you. Though I don't know if the *it* is something given. Luck and tenacity can even generate energy. I'm not at all sure. But there is a but, Nina, and there may be nothing to do about it. It can't be remedied unnaturally. Sometimes it can't be remedied naturally. The remedy may be unnatural intrusion in certain spirits.

"I speak of love."

The face so lined, so bright in eye. Which was he, great server or botching maker? Cape folded around him like furled wings. Benevolent condor. Velvet clips nuzzling the shag. "Passion," he said softly. "That which is out of Nina, and remakes Nina. Sexual passion. Love from mind to body. The human being's fire. Prometheus against the chill. Against the inhuman order. Love is the dimension killer. The source of what counts. The great act, the good state, the beautiful work. Nina, your fine work is without love."

The sun pours on Stitch's labored stones. The colors rise against the great civic labor across the water. From his stones, authority; and from his eyes, bright beyond the earth-stuff into which his body almost visibly decays.

"I do love, Mr. Stitch. I love, feel, burn. I've even felt what you talk of." Briefly. Edward, meeting himself within her. "But here I am. Not so much." A few feet of stuff, brown top, blue eyes, dots pinked in the cheek, hands on the rib cage, touching her breasts. "I go as far as I can each day."

STITCH

"Not that you are, but *what* you are, Nina. Discipline is ancillary. Love fires it. Great work is serious, absolutely. Even watching its grin in the mirror. Even in the weakness which drives it. Nina, *caranina,* the music can be planned, instrumented, played, but between silence and sound, passion must fire it into cosmos."

"Music," she said, arm out to his guided lumps of color. "It isn't natural. Our selves are enough to contend with in nature. Why keep throwing them away? Is there music only in such discard? Isn't there sufficient music in description, in perception? And isn't passion in such music?"

"Maybe, Nina. Maybe what matters is loving what's remembered. Memory is love. Unforced transmission. You and I here, Nina, my time to yours, my feeling with yours, my dim mind to your bright work. But it says, 'Dig deep, Nina. Yield, open up. Beyond effort.' You're already halfway. Beyond indifference, beyond the desire to be stone. We're with each other here, Nina. I've seen your face in clay, Nina. There's much in it I recognize, love." With his other hand on her cheek, "In your poem too, Nina. So much found, Nina. Maybe too much. Too little lost for so much found."

❦ chapter 16

THE LETTER FROM Wallie had not been opened.
The first sign: his interests were no longer hers. All right. The
children made a fuss. She stayed in the kitchen, and to his
"Hi" returned a cold "Hello." He held each of the children
until they cried release, kissed all cheeks and Quentin's little
mouth, neutrally sweet as matter before creation, rubbed
hands up and down the lengthening bodies of Brose and
Cammie, his big, dear kids, en route out of his life.

Out of sight, but within him, a fear and chill, Cressida. If
he could have purchased warmth by throwing out the day
with Sibyl, he would not have hesitated.

He put the four letters into his pocket, a heroic suspension,
and, still in the hall, took the presents out of his bag: for
Cammie, two decks of cards, bought at the Vatican (no state
tax), for Brose, an annotated copy of the *Orlando Furioso,*
for Quentin the Campanile in a watery globe, bought as he

waited for the vaporetto at Piazzale Roma. "What about Mommy?"

"It's for later." He'd debated her present off and on since Rome, then, in Padua, had stopped at the Arena Chapel and bought an expensive print of the Visitation, the colors deeper than the flaking original. It had been either that or a cheaper one of the Charity figure. He drew it from the bottom of the suitcase, and, on the children's insistence, opened it to their cries of praise and pleasure. They sure knew how to look at pictures now. "Come in, Mommy. Look what Daddy got you."

She came, drying her hands on her apron, looked at the picture he held up to deflect the children's attention from the kissless meeting between the parents, and then as she said, "It's beautiful," and seemed on the edge of turning back, he handed it to her, and she examined it closely, her face calm, or with calm imposed on it. Her eyes seemed larger—had they been weeping?—there was an exceptional quiet about her. "Got it at the Giotto place. We'll have to drive down there soon. It's just half an hour."

"Fine. See the mail?"

"Thank you, yes. Children, go on out now, lemme change and unpack." Brose and Cammie left with further thanks, maybe, thought, *hoped* Edward, thinking their parents would exchange warm hellos in their absence. "Where's Lydia?"

"Her husband's lost his job. She's helping him fill out unemployment papers."

"Oh no." Poor Signor Macchi, a tiny little fellow, worked in the Murano glass factories. Or did till now, his lungs finally burned out. These were what Sibyl called real troubles. "Hope you gave her something for him."

"Can't keep supporting them. I don't see that there's a great pile here to throw away. I give her food."

And he'd debated giving her the Charity. "She told me once if they don't pay the rent for two months, they get bounced, and she'd have to go into some bathroomless hole with the whole gang. Give her ten thousand for the rent."

"You give it to her. It's your money."

"Yes, it is." She was on the way out. "I'd hoped it would be over when I got back."

Without turning, "How easy life is for you."

The water turned on in the sink. She's just running water. He sat on the bed, hard, and put his face into the tangle of shirts and smelly underwear.

After a minute, he remembered the mail. His mother's blue scrawl, he knew it as well as her Edwardian face:

Edward darling,

Why no letter? It's three weeks or more you know how I worry. Are the children fine? What do they do in school? Do they still know Italian so well? Where do they play now it's warm? When do you come home? *Answer questions please.*

Spring season started up must give party will have Hanna do it though she's getting lazier all the time comes in at eleven leaves right after supper has almost no work. I keep house as you know spotless gets 65 a wk cd. use similar job myself.

Aunt Rach. has stones. Dorothy Sugarman passed on. Write Ben: 942 Madison.

Write! ! ! And tell children and Cressida to.

Love and xxxx,
Mother

I found two of Dad's neckties in a draw. V, L and A. I will save them for Brose.

[161]

STITCH

An alumni appeal from Chapel Hill. Then, from Noonan, the only letter—discounting memos—he'd ever received from him:

Edward, profugus—
   Attend. Maximinus, Pseudi-Galos, 1, 247: "We are compelled to wean our minds of what we are acustomed to, and in order to preserve our lives we cease to live."
   You have had a year. Are you living? I turn the other cheek. I welcome your return. To life. Up two grand, tho money's not your end. "Dare to be wise. Begin now. The man who puts off the day when he will live rightly is like the peasant who waits for the river to drain away. But it flows on." Horoce, Epissels, 1, 11, 40. Your view of old conditions your old view. Perhaps, writes the finiky Frenchman (as trans. by Moncriff) the imobility of things is the imobility of our conception of them.
   Do not whore after strange God.
                    With very best wishes to your dear family,
                              Wm. Noonan (dictated)
WN:bl

The signature was typed: "bl" must be one of his new cookies, a line of dumbness unequaled in American business life. What a confluence: ties for Brose, promised manna from Noonan. Daddy's ties. He'd gotten most of them the day before the funeral, and the shirts, two neck sizes too small; he hadn't known the old man had gone so thin, the shoes too small, sweaters, he'd given a couple away as presents, kept the brown one he had on. What distribution there would be of his clothes.
   He broke open the letter from Wallie which Cressida had placed on top, though the postmark—from Paris—was

[162]

two days later than the one from his mother. Poor Cressida. Resisting temptation. How could she make it on her own? The letter was written in a remarkably beautiful, green-inked script, full of curls and jots. What is the poor fellow hiding?

My dear Cress and Ed,
Although I suspect that you may feel disappionted in what I found out, I am rather pleased and encouraged. Now on the surface, the response is negative. Lauren Ter Wendt says there doesn't seem to be any prospect of using you immediately. However, and I'd underline this except for laziness, however, he says what I've never known him to say before, that not only do you strike him as an excellent prospect, but that he actually suggests you come out to Santa Barbara, do something else for a brief time, and then come into the opening he is confident they'll have. (I suspect it's Gilbertson who's been straining to do his civil liberties book for ten years.) More than that, he actually knows something you can do, a place you'd be needed. The question is if you'd be at all interested in it. It seems that his boys go to the Riviera Blanca Preparatory School there. I believe it's a very good one. At any rate, they're short of instructors on the upper level, particularly in the fields in which—as I indicated to him—you're best qualified, English, History, Art History, and some general Humanities course called World Thinkers. The question is would you consent to come back for the fall term which begins at the end of September? He will see that you get housing. He does not mention a specific salary, but he believes it will be in the six to seven thousand dollar range, which seems pretty good as you'll have the usual fringe benefits of such institutions. The main thing is that it wouldn't be for long, and that you could soon move in to what I think you'd enjoy and what the Foundation could use. I hope you won't be disappointed at this. Is it stupid of me to think it's almost as good as I'd hoped for?

If I'm in Venice in June, perhaps we can talk of all this, but you might write me, or Ter Wendt directly, the Hammondson Foundation, Montecito (that's a few miles south of Santa Barbara). I think the school's there as well.

With love to all of you,
Wallie

After he'd reread the letter he brought it in to Cressida, placed it on the kitchen table directly in front of a crack in the wall, and told her it was something which might interest her. He'd like her opinion. She nodded.

Twenty minutes later he went in. The letter lay in a similar —but not the same—position. "Well, what do you think?"

"I haven't had time to read it." She was sewing a skirt of Cammie's, looking out the window at the children playing *nascondo*.

He left it there, went out, took Quentin by the hand and walked slowly up the fondamenta. A beautiful day. The sun drew the colors from the Zattere, the boats, the water. The domes of the Salute floated in the air, the gulls squawked, boats swished in the canal. Familiar faces greeted him. He greeted back. Quentin was patted, tickled, kissed. The biggest twenty-month-old child in the recent history of the Giudecca, a smiler with an almost full mouth of little teeth. Edward carried him after a while, kissing him on the cheeks and under the ear, muttering his name. This was what counted. This was his out.

2

That night, after a supper across which Cressida's rapier had drawn his own out to counter, and Brose and Cammie, amidst his account of Justinian and Theodora, Sigismundo and Alberti, had felt the sharp flicks of the exchanges, Edward felt his stomach turn with the underdone tortellini. As if his body had been opened up and manipulated by Cressida's culinary viciousness. "I shouldn't have taken spring at its word," he said before dessert. "I'm getting a cold." He went off to bed, Cammie attending him sympathetically, Brose coming in later to ask if he were up to a few hands of twenty-one. He wasn't up to anything. Night lowered the temperature fifteen degrees, and entombing himself within four blankets, his teeth chattering, Edward saw a parade of the letters and the facts behind them, a parade constructed by fever which saw him and a ragged Brose facing each over a desk on a beach toward which came a school principal, Wallie, who regretted that he had to dismiss him for trifling with the girl students. Even the Alumni Office showed up in the form of the Old Well at Chapel Hill by which sat Adrienne, bleeding.

"Oh no," called Edward. Cressida appeared with a glass of water and some aspirin, her face out of sight in the dark, her hand cold and trembling as his reached for the pills. In the morning he couldn't disentangle this from the dreams.

He stayed in bed three days, the children bringing him soup and spaghetti. Once or twice Cressida came, put a tray on the chair beside his bed, and left with a nod. He asked her what he should do about Wally's proposal.

"That's your concern." How long could she keep it up, or was this what nourished her? At least she almost acknowledged having read it.

The fourth day, shaky but clearheaded, he dressed and went to see Nina. It was another beautiful day. The chairs were spread in front of the Piazza cafés, and they sat in the morning sun at Quadri's.

Nina told Edward what Stitch had told her. "He was wrong. Though there were lots of changes to make. I think I've made most of them. I'm not just crowing. I know there's not all that to what I've done. But I know he's wrong. He's always made mistakes. He told you that. Well, he made another. I don't think there was a trace of malice in it. Indeed, he prescribed a formula for recuperation," and she told Edward what it was.

He regarded her little bulldog head sipping the dark Campari-soda, licking the drops off her lips. *"Sono pronto a servirti."* Though he was outraged at the old bugger's nerve. "Maybe the old creep was removing his own britches. He'd really have you in stitches." Though you couldn't tell. "Or Stitches in you."

The Quadri band struck up. "'Twas on the Isle of Capri That I Met Her." Behind them an elderly American lady told an Italian woman about a movie made in Venice with Katharine Hepburn in which the Square was prettier than it was here.

"I resent his power with you, Nina. Maybe because he's earned it."

"Get off that."

"But who is anyone to tell anyone else she needs loving up?"

"Why is 'that' so sacred? Is it any more important than any other part of life? You're not unlike him. In that way. If that makes you proud."

Which, for a second, it did. "I wish things were parceled out better. Me with Stitch's authority or he with my—well, equipment. Life's divided up like one of these toys you put together for kids. Except the shafts are in New York, the bolts in Singapore, and they omitted the assembly plan." The American lady sang, "In the shade of an old walnut tree." Edward tapped his spoon on the water glass for the waiter. "Who can think in this racket?" he said loudly. The elderly woman stopped.

They went back to Nina's for Carlo, leashed him, then walked through crowds to the Rialto, looking into stores, buying Edward a blue foulard in Ceroni's. "For your polo coat."

Cammie's birthday was coming up. Nina found a hand-stitched linen blouse for three thousand lire. "From Burano. The Venetian eye-stitch, rediscovered after two hundred years."

"You can't get away from him," said Edward, but happy thinking how pretty Cammie would look, how she would love it.

Spend, spend. There's not much more time. He bought Nina two handkerchiefs and a slip, a pair of leather gloves for himself, a Mickey Mouse watch like Adela's for Quentin, and for Brose *Vanity Fair* from the secondhand bookstore near Campo Manin. How long would that American lady be turning over his rebuke? Pointless. No. She was a pest, a bad example, gave the nation a bad name. And if the nation had a bad name? Bellicosity flared. At the Goldoni statue they ran into, Jaska whom Edward, leaning over his packages, kissed on the mouth. She had a client on the hook coming for tea that afternoon. Would they come and look like customers? Maybe. Nina growled.

They crossed the bridge, went to the Ristorante Madonna for lunch, eating in silence, ears cocked for an Italian monologue on the cultivation of figs which a white-headed *professore* addressed to a tiny, bespectacled yes-man. They followed the sun across town to the Zattere and had ice cream under the windows where Ruskin wrote at *The Stones of Venice*. One of

[167]

the white-and-gold steamships of the Adriatic line was tugged past them to the pier. Students were out in fishing boats, others filled the cafés. Across the way, the Giudecca, gray, except where the curve below the Redentore snared a patch of sun. The Zitelle area wouldn't get any until just before dark. As they were finishing their ice cream, Stitch, in green fedora and gray cape, appeared with Miss Fry on the bridge. Nina turned her head, getting out of sight behind Edward, but he called, "Hi," and got up. "Won't you sit down?" It was the first word he'd said to them since Christmas except for the hurried "Good morning" to Miss Fry after he'd fallen down in their calle. They smiled, came up, shook hands, Stitch silently. Edward cleared the packages and Nina Carlo off chairs.

Edward forced timidity out of himself. After all, he was Stitch's host, yet, while Miss Fry and Nina discussed the weather, what they'd been doing and buying, he and Stitch sat wordless as bookends. When the ice cream came, Stitch, despite Edward's almost angry insistence, drew out his green felt change purse and paid the waiter. He downed the ice cream in six or seven ferocious gulps, then looked into Edward's eyes, his own flaring with emerald humor, and said, "And how long will you be with us?"

What a question. The ladies turned to Edward for answer. "I don't quite understand," said Edward. Did he mean at the table? Am I supposed to get up and leave now that he has taken over the poppa's chair?

For clarification, there was a smile, tinged with the mint and cherry which glazed Stitch's beard.

"I think he wonders how long we'll have the pleasure of your company in Venice," said Miss Fry, smiling.

"I haven't quite decided. My money is going fast. It's a matter of two or three months now. I don't have a job as yet. It's not as easy for us who don't have special gifts." Looking at Stitch. "You and Nina here," and then to Miss Fry, "all have gifts. I'm without them. I have to find a place."

"Ah, not me," said Miss Fry. "I'm just a servant, Mr. Gunther. Perhaps you and I could team up and make ourselves indispensable as a household combination. Except I'm sure you have many gifts. Don't you think so, Thad? Don't you think Mr. Gunther must have many gifts?"

Stitch was staring at the vaporetto coming in from San Basilio, but his head, half-turned, inclined once.

"Mr. Gunther has more literary insight than any critic I've run into," said Nina.

Edward blushed and failed an attempt to stifle a proud grin. "If reading qualifies one, I'm perhaps qualified."

"Oh no," said Miss Fry. "Nina knows how much more there is to it than that. I was always absolutely lost when these wonderful men read us their work. And yet I thought I'd read a bit here and there. But reading and affection aren't enough. I don't have a literary brain, or much of any other kind. You clearly do." Firmly, shaking her white head with each assertion, eyes smiling, a bulwark.

Yes, Stitch, they know I know values. What do you do when a mess of fine verse is put in front of your nose but shaft the poet? Some critic.

Stitch turned back to them. "I merely wondered if Mr. Gunther's grant had terminated."

"Ah," said Edward, relieved. "I thought you knew I wasn't an academic. I came on my own. I sold the house we lived in,

my kids' insurance plans, and came." Stitch nodded again, his
eyes on Edward, though Edward didn't have the feeling he
was looking at him. He forced himself another notch forward,
and said, smiling, to lessen the presumption. "I hope there's
room for the two of us here."

Stitch smiled sweetly, as if he hadn't understood but would
have liked to hear anything that could come from so wise and
good a source.

"We had better get back, Thaddeus," said Miss Fry, getting
up. "It's the Soup-Tureen's day." The "Soup-Tureen" was a
hands-on-hips, no-nonsense English woman who paid a weekly
call on what she elsewhere called "the jailbird." "Will you both
come after and take her taste out of our mouths? Do please."

Stitch rose, and so did Edward, who looked at Nina for a
cue.

"Perhaps we can," she said. "Though Mr. Gunther may have
plans."

"I'll try," he said, and took Miss Fry's hand, and then Stitch's
which was firm and accompanied by another sweet smile.

When they were out of sight, Nina said, "One thing I guess
both of us shouldn't forget, Eddy, is that he's an old man.
Older than eighty-year-olds who haven't gone through what he
has. We should just take the honor and pleasure of his presence and forget about unraveling what he says. He's just got
no serious interest in other things now. In my verse or your
presence."

It didn't serve Edward. He could not feel a serious discrete-
ness between men and old men, as he couldn't between his
children's minds—or Cressida's—and his own. Mind was mind.
The old had interests as well as the young. Of course genius
was in another category, whatever it was, and he was willing

to grant Stitch a visa through his feelings on that basis, but he would not reduce him to just another old man. Nor would he go there this afternoon; he'd had enough mind-wringing tension for one day.

3

Which did not relieve him of Stitch's question. "How long will you be with us?" General as an oracle, it furrowed into every direction: How long will the likes of you be with those of us who are serious? How long will your indirection lapse here, this most clearly directed of places, you who don't even have the resolute transience of a tourist but are little more than a fugitive? Or, how long is Nina going to have to put up with you till she gets on with what counts for her, since clearly you're not capable of giving her anything but a piece of beef? Or, when are you going to leave us alone? You're blocking the view.

When was he going to leave?

The money was enough for three or four months, but then, if there wasn't a job waiting, and he needed money for, God knows, anything, doctors, nourishment, alimony, the roof, what would happen? It was nothing to trifle with. He wasn't even a good loan risk any more. "Resigned your position and went off for a year? A legacy, Mr. Gunther? Ah no. Just fed up with things. I understand that. Often wished I could head out myself, take the wife and kids off to Samoa, lie in the sun. Never have been able to swing it." No, not a good risk. Didn't want to be. What kind of life was it that shaped itself into a good risk? "I didn't raise my boy to be no risk."

His vaporetto left Sant' Eufemia and rounded the crescent

toward the Redentore. The sun was just settling in the angle. White and gold poured out of the long stairs, the pillars, the dome. *Farmacia, Tabacchi, Macelleria, Trattoria,* the *Prigione,* the gardens of the Principessa Aspasia, fat-armed wives, over-alled men, the *Giudecchini,* children, priests, fishermen, getting their ration of afternoon sun. His own children, down the way, fishing with string and bare hook for the canal catfish. Round the bend, San Giorgio on the right, the Campanile on the left, the Salute opposite, the air blue and gold around them, the lagoon between them out to the Lido and the millennial walls. Out of this flooding danger rear the lovely towers. How long? Surely it was a proper question, whatever the reason it was asked.

chapter 17

CRESSIDA felt she was in a car that was out of control. The driver, Edward, was reckless, whether from malice or stupidity didn't matter much. If she could get a hand on the wheel, a foot on the brake, there was hope of getting out with nothing worse than a broken leg. But getting control meant getting home. She could not make it any longer here on the Giudecca. It was just not her brand of life. In the markets, the Giudecca women pushed her out of the way, shouting their orders. She had none of their insistence, none of their crude fatalism, the confidence of their poverty. Though God knows she'd better acquire some of that. The savings balance was down to a couple of thousand, and Edward was still handing out the lire left and right, paying Lydia's rent and a double salary, buying presents for the children, clothes for himself, taking five or six meals a week in town. A dark Santa Claus, though the presents—even those to others—went to himself.

When he was home, she could hardly look at him. Yet,

when he was off in one of the cars he rented for his excursions, she found herself thinking, If he crashes, what will become of us? Could she manage to get out of Italy by herself, let alone manage after that? He didn't even have life insurance any more. She would have to throw herself on McGowan's diplomatic hands; in exchange for a pinch or two, he might get her on the boat.

If she could just get back home. Back to Chicago, back on solid ground. Not with her mother, God forbid, but where she knew her way around. She'd force Edward into an income she knew he could earn. She'd get a nursemaid and go back to work herself.

But the waste and loss within this vision oppressed her. Impossible to live with, Edward had once been more than possible. Before Europe.

Europe had brought out the worst in him, culture-hunting, church-licking, you'd think he was on the verge of conversion to see him eating up the Madonnas, lecturing the kids on their inadequate grasp of Europe's greatness, then exhibiting a behavior that had about as much to do with civilization and culture as a tiger vomiting the remains of a jackal. Adultery, negligence, sloth—despite his typing—waste, getting fat again, his exercise going by the boards. Not that she cared. Let him swell up as big as San Marco.

She dusted, or started dusting off the newest addition to the house, a framed sketch of Edward Nina had done for the dreamed-up book of essays he had with maidenly blush *let out* he was writing. As if he were up to composing a children's story. He couldn't even keep his own entertained. The sketch was a monstrosity: he looked like a Nigerian sow, bristling, dark, fatter in jowl than even he'd become. That he could have accepted it, probably paid for it if she knew that scheming little poor-mouther, and then actually had it framed and nailed it—yes, he'd managed to lift a hammer for this high purpose—to the frescoed dining-room wall (over a violet hill on which Bacchus cavorted with a boy friend) was another confirmation of his European metamorphosis. Blind as well as wild, stupid as well as a sneaking chaser.

It was not going to go on. He could go out and teach children in California to be high-minded culture vultures and distribute copies of this portrait as examples of what good things came from such pursuit, but she would not be around dusting the frames. No. He'd have to moonlight a bit to keep her where she was going to be.

Poor Wallie. He thought it would all be smooth with the holy family rollicking around Europe. The bachelor's vision. Not that she wanted to blur it. Not his, nor anyone's, her mother's, even Edward's mother, that straw-brained penny-pincher who'd talked up Adrienne's virtues at her the first five years and spent the rest condemning her—Cressida's—extravagance. "You'll have all my things one day, don't see why you have to spend three hundred dollars on a couch that doesn't look half as nice as mine will ten years from now." She'd have them sleeping on the floor till she broke up the apartment she'd been abandoning each year since her husband's death.

And the children. How was she going to tell the children? Quentin's first sentence, just last week, was "Me Loves Dadda," and though he could perhaps forget, Brose and Cammie, for all the brutal treatment they took from him day in and day out, missed him when he was off on one of the trips, missed his noise, his complaints, his presence. That loud, porcine presence.

Yet it was warm, and Venice was beautiful, and her bad year

was dying along with the poor old Pope whose agonized transfiguration filled the newspapers which purveyed his cancer like a national nostrum. Once this year was over, she would force herself into an independence no one was ever going to take away from her again, no husband she would find, and no children she had or would have. The protester's reformation, she said in happy *trouvaille,* the sort of remark she used to tell Edward only to see it floating up in one of his monologues as if born in his own pure blue. Now she'd shed that German name that sounded like some horse pill laxative. Gunther's. Take it and die slow. No, sir. Life can begin again for the likes of Magruders as well as Gunthers. Signora Lydia may be stuck with her burnt-out man, but that was part of the European bargain. That was the Church, the freezing houses, the outdoor plumbing which you paid to live cheek by jowl with the Ducal Palace and the Carpaccios, not that Signora Lydia would know Carpaccio from a shoemaker. A *scarpaccio.* Yes, score two, Magruder.

Cressida started to smile, but moving her lips did something else to her, and out of some nonthought she began sobbing, so that Signora Lydia, bringing Quentin home for his midday *pappa* and *nana,* found the beautiful American lady in a terrible state and wished she could take her in her arms and ease her troubles. Though it was nice to see that having money didn't solve everything.

2

After Easter, Venice began that reflected fusion of stone, air, and water which made it the finest walking city of all. And he did walk and walk, all over the places he'd walked for sixty-nine years, even into new ones, or at least ones he didn't recognize. He'd surely never seen Sant' Andrea dei Mendicanti, not that there was much there under the gold leaf, but there it was, a church he hadn't been in. And he hadn't been in San Sebastiano since the restoration work, and old Veronese showed up beautifully, far less muggy than he'd have guessed. The restorer, like an iron shadow up on the scaffold, worked on something propped against the boards. One of his own paintings. Left hand Veronese, right hand me. A clear note of this city where the past had to be circumvented if the present were going to breathe. He felt a touch of restoration himself. Walking meant that he talked less, and talking had always been his trap. Talk, God knows, was a sea out of which many marvels came, but he had hooked more shoes than fish there. Was it the Ouan-Jin statue that had the mouth removed so it wouldn't multiply categories?

He'd been to San Giovanni in Bragora looking at Cima's John the Baptist. Poor Henry, who hadn't been able to concentrate in Venice, missed it, as he'd missed so much for all his brilliant gawking. What had Ezra said, that his Muse came to him in a corset? Venice-love was a career for fools, just as Venice-hating served the wiseacres bringing slingshots instead of eyes. But Henry was right about the colors. The pink which seemed to be everywhere was illusory. The water was green and silver where it wasn't stained tan and red from excreta. Gianbattisto Cima da Conegliano. And always painting the Baptist. Maybe this was his own affinity with him. The best of the Slotermans called him a forerunner. It could be worse. Gesù himself didn't know whether he was harbinger or follow-up

[177]

Messiah. Such claptrap. As sold by the yard in San Rocco by Cima's successor. As if subject redeemed. Or anything when form was dead.

Well, he'd done the head, and considering much, it was not negligible. No Olmec marvel, but something. In two good days he'd spotted what counted in her face. When he'd told her where the hollow was in her poem, he'd seen what counted rise up, and he'd gone home to put it into the clay. Stony force. Yes, her sources were stone, she was not touchable, for all her concessions to gentleness. Her harmony, her peace were stone. It might suffice. Less had done beautifully. Sansovino was stony. And Jane Austen.

At any rate, caught in a billowing cube, the head was something. The first in two years, almost three if you discounted the little study figures. Maybe it should go to Sant' Ilario. Tenacity as Woman. Woman standing on the world's brawn, howling to be measured with the same yardstick. With Coke, Justinian, and Hammurabi in the Compass-case under the Rememberers.

Well, he'd done it. He was not yet junk with other junk. And then, too, he'd perhaps set her straight as well. She could see its truth. Stitch the apothecary. Rx: alter thyself with amour. Maybe he would even give her the pill. Not—no, but Sloterman. Why not? She was not up to much more. As for that great rhino whose head was every now and then cracked by a thought, what could he prescribe?

Rx: Climb into the pan.

No. *Doucement. Considerate la sua semenza.* He would find something for him. *Stitch on the Conversion of Jews. On Conservation. On Reformation.*

Venice and spring were playing with him. Hardly able to

keep his own shag afloat, here he was buoying up the local flotsam. Stitch, fisher of . . .

3

Jaska, offered a one-man show in a little town just west of Mantua, has asked her clutch of foreign friends, Nina, Edward, and the Baron—back for the hunting season—to accompany her there to jack up the tone and prices. Edward and the Baron are to make introductory comments. Edward's heart chatters with fear that his thought's Italian costume will be indecent. He is to be introduced as *Professore*.

Nina goes along for laughs and the ride. It's a day off from the epic, to which she has returned with the furious impulse to secure Stitch's approval on her own terms. She does not fear a break in the rhythm; her song is within her, she can't lose it. She has her notebook along for emergency inspirations. And, too, she is once again comparatively flush. Oklahoma has sent her 350 more dollars, and she has paid debts up and down Venice. Even Bicci has been tendered some lire, and the Countess has received a monthly installment along with Carlo whom she is to tend for the day. Then, too, after work, Nina has been going into the Piazza with her sketch pad. She has made twenty portraits, including one of Edward, and received anywhere from two to ten thousand lire (Edward's) apiece. Jaska, she knows, couldn't make a nickel in such legitimate fashion. She goes along today to see the side of bacon and two photographs with the local *sindaco* which she envisages as Jaska's maximal return.

It's a merry ride. The Baron is full of witty malice, Nina,

Fabio, and Edward roar. Oskar, driving his fatigued Millecento, concentrates on the road. Their route is by autostrada to Verona and then south to Mantua. Edward has not seen Mantua. He is full of Vergil, the Mincio, the Mantegnas in the Ducal Palace. But they don't stop, and all he sees are the castle walls hulking over the shallow river. A few kilometers west is San Anselmo, a spurt of faded ambition coagulated into a tower, a church, and a clump of orange and ash-gray houses rising in the green plain beside the Po. "Dante calls it 'Po.' Without the article." Edward to Nina.

Yes, she thinks, her portrait of him was just. The swiller of dry pods. Not that she had come out much better in Stitch's hands. That unveiling—*sans voile*—at last week's tea rocked her, and had it not been for the blow she'd taken on Sant' Ilario, it would have rocked her more. The same opinion but this time visible, attached to the indubitable, masterly facts of her beclayed features. He had made her into a kind of come-hither Celt. She did not pretend to beauty, but her face must show something more than he'd found there. He had made her look mechanical, abstract, device-like. The facial planes were in themselves far more handsomely evident than her own, but this misattribution of virtue only made it worse. It was as if he thought she'd labored for her face. As if the machine devised nothing but its appearance. It would have been right for Jaska.

In the little town piazza, there is a small crowd, jacketed and befrocked, clearly out of the hills. Jaska is to be the toad of this pool. In the car she is gurgling, "What a reception. I feel like Sophia Loren. The shaved one must be the *sindaco*. Stop, Oskar. We go up *a piedi*."

It is the mayor, squat, small-toothed, courteous. He greets the distinguished and *bellissima pitrice:* it is a marvelous thing for so small a town to have a gallery, thanks to their beloved Dottore Bonmiglia, and he speaks for both gallery and town in welcoming the distinguished guests. Across the square, Jaska's Venetian squashes stream from the walls of an ex-hallway into the street. Jaska tells Edward to begin his presentation.

Edward wears his blue polo coat, new foulard and flannel trousers, his cruising costume. His dark glasses resist the white spring light. He does not feel properly dressed. The dominant tone is dark; there are no sport clothes, certainly no white flannel trousers. Nina's face is coiled with amusement; her teeth are on her lip, her eyes flicker with anticipation. Jaska, large, soft, blunt, a glass of blond beer waiting for local imbibition, waits tensely. The baron eyes a farmer.

Edward steps forward, smiles, bows to the officials, his friends, the dark crescent of local attention. For a second he thinks he might get away with speaking English. No. He plunges, his oratorical debut. *"Signore, signorine, signori. Che piacere d'essere qui,"* and starts to say "with you" but cannot think of the formal "you" and stops on *"qui."* Perspiration moves from eye socket to glasses. He removes them. *"Come la Signorina"*— There is a blank at Jaska's surname, and Edward mutters "van ughsh, *sono un straniero, ma non come la bellissima signorina, non sono un pittore, non sono un artista che ha capito lo spirito d'un paese e l'ha refatto in bei quadri."* Oh, he is aloft. The glasses move up and down in his hand for emphasis. *"La Signorina come vedono, ha depinta una città ch'appartiene agli stranieri come appartiene agli Italiani. Venezia è il dono dell' Italia al mondo. E poi, la signorina,"* with a bow and smile to

Jaska, *"ha pagato il conto con questi bellissimi quadri,"* sweeping the glasses and the crowd's eyes toward the painting. *"Non sono un critico d'arte. Sono solamente come voi,"* and the familiar is out, no hackles following it, *"un conoscitore, qualqun' che ama le belle cose, i suoi lavori che fanno per nostra piacere, per nostra,"* and with another sweep, *"richezza interiore. Eccomi qua, signore, signorine, signori, venuto qui per festaggiare con voi la manifestazione artistica della nostra brillante olandese, la Signorina Jaska Van ugsh."* The glasses sweep out and there is a breeze of applause around the powerful clapping of a roaring Nina. Edward goes over to her, debates another bow, but then hears the Baron begin to talk, in accentless Italian, of the tactile values and spatial insights of Signorina Moetenkamp.

Well, it is a great relief, if not something of a triumph. Nina tells him he is born for politics.

Who knows? There are greater surprises in the world, and though no one is as aware as Edward that this triumph is set in the most parochial of contexts, no one else knows that it compares very favorably indeed with his only other public appearance, the anonymous, silent witness of the abused fence Mungelic. As Jaska flowers under the Baron's eulogy, and then as she wades in to dispose of her Venetian daubs for 5,000 lire a crack, Edward knows his own interior triumph, gained also as a foreigner although against the grain of his introspective disposition.

4

Riding back, Edward suddenly sees himself the object of an absurd self-flattery. I'm making a farce of myself. An object.

Self-reification, a form of suicide. Self-study is a trap when the self overshadows everything: the sundial eclipsing the sun.

They did not stop in Mantua. Would he ever see those Gonzaga frescoes, so local and so unlocal? What a hint. What had he been doing but hogging Italy against the imagined winter of his life? Stuffing for a feast no one would ever eat. Couldn't he lose himself in what counted, what belonged to him, what was his human duty to assist and care for? Yes, but first he had to understand what he was. A rusty, backfiring, clotted ego couldn't serve. Clean out the heart.

❧ chapter 18

To UNCLOT, clear up, strip down, how Edward tried
in his last Venetian days as June bloomed in the city and the
dustless air transmitted sunlight to the stone and water surfaces
and retransmitted reflections with beauteous precision, or, in
ruffled lagoon, with beauteous muddle. In and out among tourists skeining off the Piazza into the back streets with swollen
lumps of glass and hunks of stone hacked and muddied into
antiques, Edward walked and bumped and thought, head
furrowed with his own reflections. He told himself his years
of self-absorption had been but internal primping. Now he
must dig deep. Edward-*Sein* must find himself. Is Edward-
thinking Edward-acting? Is Edward-thinking-now Edward-
thinking-NOW? Is there an Edward-*Sein* beneath every Edward?
Fortunate *Vorsokratiker,* who had but substance to observe,
unconscious of the darkness of their own observance. Can
Edward-observing see Edward-observed? Time-bound as he is?

Germanic headachery, heidiggery, schnitzel-swill.

Basta. Noon, Nina. The Piazza, Tickets, checks, alimony, letters, Noonan, Wallie, Santa Barbara.

On a vaporetto, tight within a family of squat Berliners, instructing Poppa's pedagogical index under his nostrils, Edward corrects in his college German, *"Nein, mein Herr. Das ist doch kein Palast, aber der Fischmarkt."* Yes, he can teach the high-and-low digging schnitzlers a few tricks.

In Bicci's garden, to Nina, "I'm the type who should work with a good institution." Puggish, wordless interrogation over tomato and eggplant. "Because I haven't a talent to be proud of, I keep leaning on other people. If I were Gunther of the AP or Gunther of Health, Education and Welfare, I'd have something, I'd be something."

"You're one of God's chosen, and you spend half your time complaining about it. Relax. Enjoy your many enjoyments."

"They get in each other's way."

"American, thirty-five, a good daddy, educated, vacationing in Venice, you're what the luxury state's all about. Let alone the neo-Freudians."

The sun filtered through a fig tree, mottling Nina's face. How I'll miss it, thought Edward. I'll miss everything. Here I go again. What an onion. Stripping down and there's no core left. Maybe it's why Stitch gets to me: he does the stripping for me. And the only truth that counts for me is harsh. "Nina, we're like onions, roses. There's no core to us."

"Can't you tell an onion from a rose?"

Yes, he'd overlooked that. Though he'd stripped down so much he didn't know whether he was one or the other. You had to get outside yourself to find your shape. The Archimedean point. Three days would see him on the *Saturnia* taking off with Cress and the children for two months with Noonan in Chicago and then, by himself, to Santa Barbara for the "trial separation." Europe had not located the point for him.

Yet there was a local Archimedes. Instant knowledge dispensed, Calle Ramigero, 5:30 to 6. If he could only see him once more. One word could do it. Between the stirrup and the ground. He would not meet his like again. "Nina, I need to see Stitch before I go."

Nina regarded his dark monkish pate shadowed with little spade-shaped leaves. No laurels on this earnest, inquisitive, consumer's face. "Why not? Write him a letter if you want. He's no spook."

He did, then and there, and slipped it under the door in Calle Ramigero: would they have dinner with him and Nina (for safety, for insurance) tomorrow in Bicci's?

2

Dear Mr. Gunther,

How nice of you to think of us. We have thought often of you, and only TS's uncertain condition has prevented our asking you here. Now he seems better, and although I don't think we can take the chance of accepting your delightful invitation to come out, we would be so happy if you could stop in for tea, at five o'clock, and stay for a half hour or so. Do bring Mrs. Gunther if you can. I hope Nina will be there as well.

Cordially,
Lucia Fry

Edward read it standing amidst a photographing mob, some of whom recorded his flushing pleasure. "So you're invited?" said Nina.

Yes, they wanted him. Not the same as their having dinner with him, but something. (Why should the old man never take anything from him?)

That afternoon he rode the boats up and down the canal, saying good-by to the palaces and churches. Jammed up against a lovely French girl in short shorts, he had an idea. *"Voudriez-vous m'accompagner à Torcello pour voir les mosaics. Elles sont les plus importants du nord d'Italie."*

A stare of amused contempt. *"Je ne parle pas italien, monsieur. Je ne parle que français."*

A beatnik-viper. Never had Edward seen himself reflected in such fashion, balding comic lecher. It was so crowded, he couldn't move away from her, and she didn't bother to move. Her bare legs excited him even as his heart thumped with her rejection. It's good for me. Yes. It's just the ticket for me. At last. The harshness of truth.

3

In the straw chair, green eyes in the heavy head fired from currents unavailable elsewhere.

"Mr. Stitch, I thought I'd just say good-by. You'd wondered when I was heading off. I suppose—things being what they are—I won't see you again. So I thought I'd, well, take advantage of what's a rare opportunity on earth, knowing a wise man—"

"Won't find wise men elsewhere, but you're barking up the wrong tree here." And, tapping the gray shag, "Mare's nest."

"Maybe, but it'll do." Low in the canvas chair in which he'd been humiliated Christmas Day. Unnecessarily. Two men in a little room with a bit of Venetian spring coming in the window, talk and boat noises from the fondamenta. Miss Fry rattling plates downstairs. A couple of men. In a million years who would distinguish one from the other? But now, *subito*.

Could he ask "What should one do?" Like the man who asked Morgan about the yacht, if you had to ask, don't. But, with Stitch's smile hooking into him, he blurted, "What's it all about?" Retract. Unretractable. In his polo coat, green gabardines, Italian moccasins.

The heavy head leaned, the green eyes stared into Edward's. "Holes and fillers. Stars-space, men-women, bodies-graves. Core of Ilario's a hole."

This was too remote. Where could he find a leverage point here? It was just such abstraction that must have driven Stitch into the inferno for ten years. Bulldozing trees to build his highway. "Must be more than that."

Stitch raised a hand to his forehead and, squeezing, doubled up the wrinkles. His eyes flared, flickered, he opened his mouth, but no sound issued.

Outside of Miss Fry's pound cake and jasmine tea, and then the old man's farewell smile, Edward got nothing more than that.

He took the traghetto over the canal for the last time. Spring dusk, gold struts, colored whorls, douce lights in the canal, a depth of sadness in this tunnel of love. There had been no knightly investiture. No message. No leverage point. Stitch's smile meant more than any words, meant they were in the same boat.

Disembarking, he heard the Campanile bells. It wasn't the hour: no other campaniles took it up. My God, had Stitch gone to fill his hole? With his last words for me. I should call the AP.

At Nina's, tears told him the bells were for the old Pope. "I'm going to the church. What a man he was."

Edward walked with her. In the Piazza, television sets sprouted in the dark. Which was that night's only Venetian service, for San Marco's was locked up.

So their last hour was neither in church nor bed. It turned out there was little left to say over the coffee and the melancholy telecasters.

She walked him to the vaporetto and kissed him good-by. "We'll keep in touch." Though there'd be no need. She would inherit the spherical cousin whom Stitch was putting her on to. But she'd miss this one. Going, going, sacred and secular friends. The human burden.

❦ chapter 19

THE GAP OPENED when the taxi turned the corner, and he knew even with the relief that it was now done that he and Cressida had torn apart something living. Quentin's "Bye, dadda," as if for an afternoon, and Brose and Cammie, knowing more—that he'd be gone "until things got settled out there" —nervous, unsure of their feelings, sorry, but troubled by not feeling sorrier. Or so he felt. As for Cressida, who knew? He kissed her good-by on the cheek, "for form," "for the children," and wondered, in flash, did her stiffness soften?

When the fan-jet rose to 31,000 feet beyond Denver, the gap widened. Years of secondhand knowledge and 31,000 denaturing feet did not close it. For the next hour civilization did not exist. Mountains, sugar-topped lumps of chocolate pudding, canyons, a scoriasis of the earth skin, then the undulant, dead beauty of the deserts. Los Angeles was great relief: people, trees, cars, streets, houses, wild white buildings, meshed, glassed, the new tropic, open to space, the sea, the air, its forms lunar, stellar.

The shack in Montecito was on the ocean. Half the day the

tide crashed against the stone foundation, rattled the wooden pillars holding the balcony, which every morning was dark with spray. The property of Ter Wendt of the Foundation, it hung over the public entrance to the beach, an asphalt descent used by the surfers who poured in whenever the tide was right. They needed precious little, beyond waves and a few feet of launching sand. When Edward woke up at six to the noise of the water roaring like monster reams of paper ripped by monsters, there they would be, boys and girls from twelve to thirty, golden, muscular, eyes on the ocean, the sleek boards on their heads or under their arms or knees as they dog-paddled out sixty yards to stand over the rolling waves and ride like Roman emperors into perilous finales near a spine of rocks angled from the beach. Usually they were silent, but on shore, waiting in a stone ingle or on the sand, they exchanged some sort of speech Edward could hardly make out, hip formulas about waves and weather. They never really smiled, though they were full of quick grins, their teeth flashing out of dark faces. Some of them slept in beat-up station wagons: coming from school, Edward would see bare feet and a surfboard sticking out the back, an oddly amorous coupling.

Occasionally there was a ruckus. It could start with one of the strange formulas which would be scratched up on the stone wall with the burnt ends of wood (they often built fires). The first day two girls got into a fight when an incomprehensible exchange of what Edward could only guess were words flamed into action. A girl with red hair grabbed a piece of wood and printed CHOLPAS MAC KNUKKY on the yellow wall among the other slogans and initials. The other girl, a platinum blonde with a harelip, screeched, tore off her blonde hair from which tumbled a mass of black, and went for the redhead, pushing and punching her in the arms and chest. The redhead scratched a little and then ran up the road over the single-gauge railroad track and disappeared.

Usually, though, it was calm, even bland.

Which is the way Edward found everyone: waitresses, policemen, grease monkeys (Ter Wendt had lent him a '57 MG coupé in a package deal with the house), cashiers, the settled inhabitants of the beach, his pupils; all smiled, were polite, bland. Unless something didn't go quite right. Unless he didn't fill out the day's attendance report or go out the right door of the grocery. Then there was puzzlement, and sometimes anger.

The vegetation too was bland; much greener than he expected, though in his two months there it hadn't rained once. The place glittered with sprinklers. Day and night, spray arced lawns and soaked flowers. Which were gorgeous. Bougainvillaea empurpled a fifty-yard hedge, tuberose yellow and pale-blue flowers cupped air in every patch, the palms stretched like immense furled umbrellas, confident they'd never need to be unfurled. Everything showing, thought Edward. No roots to speak of.

At first, after a week of terrible loneliness in which he thought of nothing but Brose, Cammie, Quentin, and Cressida, he just floated, a released balloon. Except for driving up the purple hill to school, putting in seven blank hours of talking, questioning and marking, and driving back toward the sea, he had no obligations, and except for one duty cocktail party given by Ter Wendt and two teas at the headmaster's house, his time was blank. He blanked with it, obeyed no schedule of meals, rising, walking, washing. Mostly he stared at the Pacific, or walked along it. Every once in a while he wrote a letter to one of the children, ending with "Give everyone a big hug and kiss from Your Daddy," but for two weeks he received no mail at all except for "Free Gift Coupon Inside" envelopes addressed to Occupant, 502 Miramar Beach. He ate almost nothing, lived off bread, peanut butter, and cans of apple and pineapple juice. Since the house bills went to Ter Wendt, and he had a Standard credit card for gas, the first four weeks went by on the $80 cash he'd brought with him on the plane. He sent his school check to the First National Bank in Chicago where he and Cress had a joint account. He hardly thought about it, though once he told himself with some pride that he was going to manage somehow, even teaching. Then he remembered Adrienne's alimony and drew the $200 from his savings. The next day he went to Ter Wendt to tell him the problem of his three households.

Ter Wendt was a portly man of fifty-three with gentle blue eyes, a kind of human dessert. He regarded Edward with what appeared to be sympathy and said that he preferred both teachers and Foundation members to be settled. He'd believed Edward was settled.

"I was," said Edward. His chair was higher than Ter Wendt's and the man had a particularly short torso, so that Edward felt he was looking down at him from a great distance.

Looking up the same distance did not seem to perturb Ter Wendt. "Still, you clearly need money or you'll be driven frantic and not perform effectively in any sphere." Edward nodded. "I can't think of a source other than the Foundation, unless you might be willing to write book reviews for some of the newspapers around L.A."

STITCH

Edward said that as an extra chore he'd enjoy it, but couldn't take it on unless it served his financial purposes.

Ter Wendt said he'd make inquiries, and meanwhile Edward should write up a proposal for a study of some sort. The Foundation might be able to see its way clear to a couple of thousand which would "take care of some of your rather overwhelming responsibilities."

A week passed, and Edward could think of nothing at all to propose. He continued to float, to live on almost nothing. Indeed, he thought of nothing purposeful outside of getting up to school, skimming the class texts, and thinking in the ten minutes' recess after one class what he would do in the next one.

Ten days after his talk with Ter Wendt, he received his first two letters. They came on the same day, as if the post office finally decided that he justified delivery service. The first was a one-pager from Cammie.

Dear Daddy,

We are all fine, though we miss you very much. Peggy Muncie is my best friend this year. Brose is Charles' still!!! Quentin said last night, "When Dadda comma home inna taxi. Me lova him." He's getting to speak real good. I miss you too. All is fine. oooo and xxxxx,

Cammie

Edward tried not to think about this letter. The second was from Wallie.

12 rue Moncorgé
Oct. 12, 1963

My dear Edward,

I came back this evening from a short trip to Venice and found a letter from Ter Wendt which has shaken me terribly. I can't be-

[194]

lieve that the separation of two people such as yourself and Cressida—not even thinking of the darling children—can endure. I can hardly endure to think of it. If I thought that my suggestions or actions had a thing to do with it, I could not function. Yet I both must function and continue to fear that I played some part in it. I will do anything you ask me in the way of intervention or help. I have money; it's at your disposal. Eight thousand dollars. It is yours for the asking. Please write me immediately of anything I can do.

I can hardly intrude my own news at this point, but I will, because it will interest and perhaps please you. The news is that I am, in a way, engaged. "In a way," because there are certain conditions laid down by my almost-fiancée, who, I'm proud to say, is Nina. Perhaps you did not know that it was Mr. Stitch himself who introduced us. I have gone down to Venice every other weekend since you left and I offered my hand this weekend. To my delighted surprise, I was not refused. I will tell you the somewhat odd but completely understandable conditions which this brilliant, beautiful, gifted girl laid down, although I am of course not anxious to have them generally known.

She says that she has a sort of aversion to corpulence. I am, as you well know, no string bean. I agreed to take off thirty-five pounds and yet keep up my—I think—good physical condition. I am about to write to the Metrecal Company in London ordering a suitable quantity of their product, and I am going to begin horseback riding and gymnastic work this week. It is something I should have done on my own, but I have always been negligent of it, perhaps because my general appearance is really unredeemable.

Dear Edward, please forgive my telling you at such a moment in your life about such a moment in mine. And please let me hear immediately from you about what I can do. I have also written to Ter Wendt about his suggestion that you do some sort of a study,

saying that no one, in or out of the academy, would be better
qualified for certain general studies.

With deepest affection,
Wallie

P.S.
I must add a piece of wonderful news just received from Venice.
Nina writes that the first Canto of her long poem has been accepted
for publication by both the *Partisan Review* of New York and—in
her own translation—by *Il Verri* of Milan. I know that she would
want you to know.

This letter, too, Edward could not bring himself to digest.
Around him the world was organizing. Peggy and Cammie,
Brose and Charley, Quentin and fatherlessness, Nina and
Wallie, though that sounded like a cruel joke of Nina's. Was
she using him as a reserve fund? Financial and sexual, in case
Stitch's prescription turned out to be right? Poor Wallie. Still,
he had hope. Which was more than he, Edward, had in this
rootless jungle, this launching platform for interspatial life.

Yet the beauty of the place calmed him. At night the water
rushed almost to his fingers, the waves lapping each other,
the foam full of sea odors and the perfume of jasmine and
honeysuckle from the gardens. Dizzy with their glory, Edward
would stare at the sea or at the star-choked dark, half-feeling,
half-thinking, What else? What else counts on this beauteous,
troubled dot? What can public or private misery do to this?

Now and then loneliness, which for a while was so thick in
him he was terrified and tearful, yielded to a girl, someone sun-
ning in a bikini under the balcony to whom he'd call down and
sometimes succeed in getting into the house. One girl, a plain
blonde with a fine, muscular body, a teacher at another private
school, came up every day for two weeks. Then, without ex-

planation, she disappeared. No phone call, nothing. For days after that Edward returned from school in a terrible depression. He could not keep out of his head what he'd sworn not to think of, the children and Cressida. He called their names out loud, pretended they were in the room, kissed the pillow as if he were kissing them, and then cried. Once he smacked his head against the green boards of the upstairs room until he felt blood there.

In early November there was another windfall. He was watching a blue yawl sailing into the bay when he noticed that a plump, pretty woman sitting on the beach next to a boy about Brose's age was staring up at him. There was something familiar about her. Edward went into his bedroom, changed into his bathing suit and came out again, holding his stomach in, tensing his muscles. The woman looked up at him again. "I know your face," he called to her, "but I can't put a name to it."

The woman got up, smiling, and Edward remembered. It was a girl, Elsie Something-or-other whom he'd known in high school twenty years ago. She'd known him right away she said, "Though like me, you've swelled up a little." She was divorced. The boy was her only child, she worked as a secretary out at the University, had rooms in Goleta. It was the first time she'd tried this beach in four years here. What a happy coincidence.

They met that night and then every night. The boy was used to being alone; she drove down from Goleta after he was in bed. They stayed in the house, drank, talked, listened to records, and made love. In a week, it felt as if they'd been together for years. The lovemaking was not extraordinarily passionate; nor was it particularly soothing. Yet it went deep, full of memory and forgotten hope.

On the two weekends they spent together, they took the boy

with them on trips, the first up the coast to see Hearst's European bargain basement, then down to L.A. where Edward wanted to see two things, Venice and the Watts Towers about which he'd read in a *National Geographic* in the school library.

He drove over to Venice by himself while Elsie and the boy went shopping in Beverly Hills. On Windham Street he parked at a meter under a filthy version of the Piazza loggia. A thin pale man with an inflamed ravine across his cheek and chin stared at him. The man's chin was linked to his lips by a bridge of brown spittle. His eyes, the same worn, gristled, yet liquid color, made another sort of bridge with Edward's. Inquiry? Bafflement? Fear? Hatred? Or brotherhood? Edward, here to look for something else, he hardly knew what, felt his quest fouled by it. With an effort like smashing a mirror, he broke the ocular bridge, then regarded the street, the exhausted, green loggia whose cement pillars gushed into identical, cretinous heads. Past filthy, dollar-a-night hostels and stores whose windows were paper rages of discounts, sales, last-weeks-in-business, Edward walked. Business. The deadest deadbeat area he'd ever seen. The deadbeats' faces were as dead as the cement ones, their clothes like bandages on their bleeding lives. Above them, the parodies of Venice, blunted trilobe windows, an inchoate Ca' d'Oro, a desert-colored Palazzo Ducale with four cement lions on its corners.

What was behind this repulsive obeisance? Here in California, over the ocean, the huge mountains, the deserts, canyons, here in this made-up land by the water, Italian-soaked, Spanish-charted, thickened with Jews, Negroes, the retired and sick, Venice extracted a final tribue.

The Watts Towers were something else. They stretched over

a scrub of slum by single-gauge tracks which came from and went nowhere. Broken tiles, chipped glass, cracked mirrors, seashells, volcanic rocks, Seven-Up bottle caps shone out of the mortared flesh of steel bed frames, spiraled, looped, and whirled into the rainbowed shapes of the Italian immigrant's thirty-year dream. Edward, Elsie, and Fritz, the boy, spent hours looking at the scallopped walls, the heart shapes, the slabs of tool forms, the stupas of chipped glass, the ships, hearths, pyramids, and minarets gathering, splitting, refracting, and fusing the California light. A one-man cathedral of love, the illiterate's Sant' Ilario. Not marble and stone rousted from the quarries of Europe for a stone epic of Western life, but its ashcan leavings.

The third weekend, the one before Thanksgiving, they planned to drive over the desert to Las Vegas.

On Friday, there was inventory-taking at the school, and Edward stayed home correcting mid-term exams on the American Revolution. At noon he heard screaming outside his bedroom window. Two girls of sixteen were rolling around on the asphalt descent to the beach, mauling each other, pulling hair, scratching. Edward, horrified, yelled at them to cut it out, though as they continued to flail away, breasts crushing each other, backs ripped and bloodied on the stone, he felt terrific desire rising in him. "Cut it out or I'll call the cops." The girl on top looked up, and he recognized her, the harelip who'd worn the blonde wig. "Get out of here," he yelled into her wounded face. Yet he wanted to say, "Let's have it out in here." The girl regarded him with blank savagery, then got up, not looking at the other one, picked up her surfboard from the asphalt and carried it up the hill. Her opponent rose and followed. Edward, dizzy, nauseous, stared at their bloodied, golden backs. Then he went into the kitchen, made himself a peanut-butter sandwich and opened a bottle of Diet-Rite Ginger Ale.

The telephone rang, Elsie telling him to turn on the television set, Kennedy had been shot dead.

That night, she did not come, only telephoned to say she couldn't; the next night, it wasn't necessary to call. Edward spent three and a half days in front of the set. When visual reception died under the marine pressures of night, he watched the sandy screen while the audio blasted. On Monday he called the school to say he wouldn't be coming in; there was no one there.

From the first hours, after the first shock wave had passed, it was clear to Edward that what had happened in Texas had to do with everything that had happened to him. It really struck him when he heard the first surfers the next day. They made the same bird noises, their shark boards still zoomed in over the waters; nothing had changed for them. The water was here, the sun was out, the tide was in. What did they have to do with what happened? With what ever happened? Their stock of the past was like the birds', corralled into a few instincts plus a few syllables, automobiles, cans. Their memory was yesterday's waves. Reality was what was in your sights. The past was what you desired right now. Was it what Stitch was getting at, what made him so gloomy? The present didn't exist because it was its own past. Was this what he meant by the death of Europe? The death of transmission? Of memory?

Monday, the funeral day, Edward watched the procession to the Capitol and heard the gruesome speeches in the Rotunda.

Then, watching the widow and her daughter come to the flag-draped coffin and the white-gloved hand of the little girl reach up and touch it, the misery not only of the moment but of his own broken life poured in him like the tide outside the window, wave after wave, so intense it paralyzed his tear ducts, made bone of his heart. His eyes on the screen, he could no longer differentiate the events. He sat for an hour as if he himself were under the draped flag, then telephoned Chicago.

Cammie picked up the phone. In the background he could hear the same noise that came off his screen.

"It's Daddy, darling. Are you watching?"

She screamed to everyone that it was Daddy. "Yes, yes, we're watching. We've all been crying. Did you see everything, Daddy? The shooting? Everything? Isn't it terrible? We've been watching all three days."

He could hear Brose yell, "Four."

"Four. Are you all right, Daddy? When are you coming?"

"I'm all right, darling. It's why I called. I'm coming soon."

"Oh, good. Goodie. Daddy's coming soon."

He heard Brose say, "Let me speak." Then Cammie, "Here, Daddy, it's Brose. I'm so glad, Daddy. It's so hard watching without you."

"Hello, Dad. Hi."

"Hi, sweetheart. How are you?"

"Just fine. All fine. I mean if you can be all fine when something like this happens." Brose was climbing the ladder, the words a bit in advance of the feelings. Still, he was a boy of fine feeling. "Are you coming home soon?"

"Yes, darling. I miss you all very much. Is Quentin there? I'd better not take too long."

[201]

"Quentin," called Brose. "Here, it's Daddy. No, like this," and a loud, "Hi, Dadda."

"Quentin darling, it's Dadda. How are you?"

"I fiuhn."

"I miss you so, darling. I'll see you soon."

"Hi, Dadda."

"Sweetheart, let me talk to Mommy, but first say good-by to me."

"I new toy, Dadda. Big 'loon."

"I'm glad, sweetheart. You play nicely with it. Is Mommy there?"

The phone crashed on the floor or against the table. Edward could see the whole room, see where the receiver could fall, hear the TV, imagine the kids restored in front of it now, Brose with legs crossed, Cammie lying on her stomach watching what he, turning, could watch, the Mass for the dead. The phone was picked up, and Cressida said in a voice into which normality was forced, "Hi. You been watching? Isn't this the worst?"

"Yes, Cress. It's what's brought me to call, I guess. When I saw the kids. His kids. I couldn't. I can't go on like this."

"Just a minute," and he heard, "Children, I want you to take Quentin out for a few minutes and play. Daddy and I have something to discuss and I can't hear while the machine's on. It's only going to be the Mass anyway. Go get some air. Go on, now, let's go. Fast. This is long-distance. Quentin, you go play now with Brose and Cammie. Go for a nice walk."

Pause. Edward could see the whole thing, the way each of them walked, Quentin in little corduroy pants and Buster Brown shoes, Cammie putting on his blue jacket downstairs in the rented house, though he could not remember from his own weeks there whether they kept their coats in the downstairs closet.

"All right now," said Cressida, her voice altered now, colder. "That's all I wanted to say, Cress. I think it's wrong. I know the wrong's been me. I want to come back. I can work with Noonan, at least till I find something else. I know offhand of a couple of things. I know it won't be easy for you, but I want to come back for you as well as the children."

There was the sound of a large breath-taking filling the empty wire, a long pause, and then she said, "Edward, you think you can always change the way things are. You're the winds and the rest of us are sails. You're moved now by this business here. We all are. But it doesn't have anything to do with you and me. We've had our funeral. It's not because I'm not tempted. This is miserable for me. It's terribly hard taking care of three children without a husband. That poor woman's going to find out." The screen showed the woman in black, Edward wanted to, but did not ask what channel she was watching. "She'll find out how to do it. Like I am. You just—"

"Cress, listen. I'm not dead. There's a big difference. Just think of the kids, if not us."

"Don't you think I did all that thinking? Don't you think I spent a year doing that thinking? The thinking's done. Can't you get that into your head?"

"Please. Please. Think again. I'm going to come home. We'll discuss it face to face."

"No!" Shouted. "No. Do you want to break the kids in half? They're just about getting used to it. No, you can't. Even for yourself. Wait till summer. We'll explain it all. I've been seeing, well, you don't know him, but he's a lawyer. I've been seeing him, and he's helping me."

So. Already. She had her man picked out, a lawyer. A package deal. When she wanted meat, she'd be seeing the butcher.

"Good-by, Cress."

"I'm sorry, Edward. Really, in my heart, deep within it, I'm sorry, but right. I'm right. We are no longer possible. We are poison. There is no point. I'm just beginning to be free."

"I'm glad for you, Cress. Good-by."

"Good-by."

Edward shut off the television set and went outside. It was chilly, but after a few minutes walking on the shore he didn't feel it. There were no waves, and so there were no surfers. The tide was low, the spine of rocks divided the sand from the water. It was among these he walked, stepping from rock to rock, hands in his pants pockets, shivering. He kept shaking his head, muttering to himself, not words, not groans, something in between. He identified with the rocks, it was a comfort. He was a rock, one of billions, formed but unformed, solid but useless, part of an ugly, spinelike nonspine, somewhere or other. His children, his beloved, precious children. What would they be told? Daddy would not be coming quite yet. He was sick. Next month. No, the summer, and then, visits. Yes, there would be those. Three households and no family. Elsie. No, no, he'd had it. No. Quentin. If he had a gun. If he had courage. If the water weren't so cold. If he could keep even miserable long enough.

He walked back and forth on the shore till he was exhausted, then went back to the house and slept on the couch.

When he got up it was close to dusk. He turned on the television set. They'd resumed normal telecasts. He shut it off. He wasn't hungry. He couldn't read. He thought of taking a drive, maybe to Elsie's, but he didn't want to leave the couch. He turned around on it, knelt and stared at the water. If the window were higher, if there weren't sand underneath. Oh, Cressida. Oh, Quentin. Oh, Cammie. Oh, Brose darling. A small green bird flew past his window and then out toward the ocean. He watched it till he could not distinguish it from the darkening air.